Paris Tales

For Anne-Marie

Paris Tales

Stories translated by

Helen Constantine

UNIVERSITY PRESS

OXFORD

UNIVERSITY PRESS

Great Clarendon Street, Oxford OX2 6DP

Oxford University Press is a department of the University of Oxford.
It furthers the University's objective of excellence in research, scholarship,
and education by publishing worldwide in

Oxford New York

Auckland Bangkok Buenos Aires Cape Town Chennai
Dar es Salaam Delhi Hong Kong Istanbul Karachi Kolkata
Kuala Lumpur Madrid Melbourne Mexico City Mumbai Nairobi
São Paulo Shanghai Taipei Tokyo Toronto

Oxford is a registered trade mark of Oxford University Press
in the UK and in certain other countries

British Library Cataloguing in Publication Data

Data available

ISBN 0-19-280574-6

2

Typeset in Minion by
Footnote Graphics Limited, Warminster, Wilts
Printed and bound in Great Britain by
Biddles Ltd, King's Lynn, Norfolk

Acknowledgements

I am very grateful to my family and my friends for their encouragement and many useful suggestions; to one or two people in particular who read the typescript and commented helpfully; to David Constantine for translating the poem in *Rue du Commerce* by Jacques Réda; to Olivia McCannon for her photographs; and to my dear friend Anne-Marie Turrel, who was my companion in Paris for so many years.

Publisher's Acknowledgements

Guy de Maupassant, 'La Nuit', *Contes et Nouvelles,* 11, Gallimard, 1979; first published in *Gil Blas,* 1881, and collected in *Mademoiselle Fifi,* 1882 and 1883.

Gérard de Nerval, 'Le Monstre vert', in *Œuvres Complètes*, 111, Gallimard, 1993; first published under the title 'Le Diable vert' in *La Silhouette,* 1849.

Honoré de Balzac, 'Le Dernier Napoléon', *Œuvres Diverses*, 11, Gallimard 1996; first published in *La Caricature,* 1830.

Émile Zola, 'Les Squares', *Contes et Nouvelles*, Éditions Fasquelle et Gallimard, 1976; first published in *Le Figaro,* 1868.

Guy de Maupassant, 'Une aventure parisienne', *Contes et Nouvelles*, 1, Gallimard, 1974; first published in *Gil Blas,* 1881, and collected in *Mademoiselle Fifi*, 1882 and 1883.

Colette, 'Le Cimetière Montmartre', in *Œuvres*, 11, Gallimard, 1996; first published in *Le Matin*, 1913; 'Flore et Faune de Paris', in *Œuvres*, Gallimard; first published in *Paysages et Portraits*, Flammarion, 1958.

Michel Butor, 'La Gare Saint-Lazare', *Illustrations*, Gallimard, 1964.

Léon-Paul Fargue, 'XXième', in *Les Vingt arrondissements de Paris*, Fata Morgana, 2002.

Julien Green, 'A Notre-Dame', in *Paris*, Éditions du Champ Vallon.

Maryse Condé, 'Portrait de famille', in *Le Cœur à rire et à pleurer*, Éditions Robert Laffont, 1999.

Georges Perec, 'Les Lieux d'une fugue', in *Les Cahiers du Sens*, Le Nouvel Athanor, 1996.

Roger Grenier, 'Une maison Place des Fêtes'.

Andrée Chedid, 'La joyeuse mort de Fassola', in *Mondes, Miroirs, Magies*, Flammarion, 1988.

Didier Daeninckx, 'L'Homme-tronc', in *Main Courante*, Éditions Verdier, Lagrasse, 1994.

Jacques Réda, 'Rue du Commerce', in *Châteaux des courants d'air*, Éditions Gallimard, 1986.

Jean Echenoz, 'L'Occupation des sols', in Éditions de Minuit, 1988.

Annie Saumont, 'Iéna', in *Le Lait est un liquide blanc*, Julliard.

Cyrille Fleischman, 'L'Aventure', in *Rendez-vous au métro Saint-Paul*, Le Dilettante.

Anna Gavalda, 'Petites Pratiques germanopratines', in *Je voudrais que quelqu'un m'attende quelque part*, J'ai lu.

Frédéric Beigbeder, 'Manuscrit trouvé à Saint-Germain-des-Prés', in *Nouvelles sous ecstasy*, Gallimard (Folio), 1999.

Hugo Marsan, 'En double aveugle', in *Festival de la Nouvelle et du Conte à Saint-Quentin 2000*, Ville de Saint-Quentin, Direction de la Culture et de l'Animation, Bibliothèque Municipale Guy de Maupassant.

Vincent Ravalec, 'Du pain pour les pauvres', in *Recel de batons*, Le Dilettante, 1995.

Contents

* The numbers in boxes indicate the locations of the individual Tales. See map on pages 244–245.

Picture Credits

Introduction

I remember the first time I visited Paris I was fascinated by the names of streets, métro stations, squares, and monuments. The Gare Saint-Lazare, the Champs-Élysées, Château d'Eau, Réaumur-Sébastopol, the Rue du Chat Qui Pêche, and the Rue des Blancs-Manteaux have always seemed much more exciting to me than, say, Kings Cross or Regent Street. I know that many lovers of Paris share my fascination, and this anthology is for them. It is a collection of short stories set in different areas of Paris, about Parisians and the places they live in.

It is well known that short stories have, until recently, been the poor relation of the novel in the judgement of serious critics on both sides of the Channel. Publishers have been wary; their usual cry: they don't sell! Yet, paradoxically, short stories enjoy great popularity with the reading public, and today the genre seems to be going through something of a revival. Elizabeth Fallaize, in her recent anthology, has suggested some reasons why this might be so. She points to the way in which the prestige of the story has been raised by the awarding of prizes by the Académie Française and Goncourt—there are now almost 120 annual short-story competitions in France—and the re-establishing of several literary magazines willing to publish them. It is also thanks to the work of Annie Mignard, whose book *La Nouvelle française contemporaine* is a treasure-house of information about the state of the genre today, and to such publishing houses as the deservedly popular Librio, who have brought out a wide selection of new stories at low prices and made them generally available in bookshops. In France the Festival de la Nouvelle in Saint-Quentin, where short-story writers meet the public (and schoolchildren in particular), organizes workshops to promote and popularize the genre.

Could another reason for this revival in popularity, not only in France but very much in Anglophone writing as well, be that we are more appreciative of the intensity, the brevity of shorter fiction nowadays? Do we prefer the suggestion to the explanation, the significant moment to the narration of a whole life, the possibilities rather than the finality, the open-endedness rather than the 'closure'? In her 1936 introduction to the *Faber Book of Modern Short Stories*, Elizabeth Bowen, greatly influenced by Constance Garnett's translation of Chekhov's stories, spoke of shortness as a positive quality; elsewhere she indicates the 'inchoate or nebulous' nature of many short stories, as though in that quality also they are closer to real life. Virginia Woolf mentions the 'note of interrogation' and the 'evanescent moment'. More recently Ian Reid has remarked: 'Complexity and breadth . . . are not always the most central or interesting feature of our lives . . . and the short story can move us by an intensity which the novel is unable to sustain.'

Some of these 'Paris Tales', for example those by Grenier, Gavalda, Echenoz, and Chedid, conform to this model. Elsewhere, as in the stories by Julien Green and Jacques Réda, the emphasis is more on the evocation of place. In them, the writers deliberately attempt to conjure up the spirit of the location, whereas in the former it may play a lesser, but nonetheless important, role. Anna Gavalda's narrator implies that her encounter would not have happened anywhere except in Saint Germain. Daeninckx's story about the events of 1968 is inextricably linked to the Latin Quarter, and so is Beigbeder's dramatic vision of another revolution. Nerval's story, set in the Catacombs, is an amalgam of fairy tale and *conte parisien*. The sergeant's bottle is described in the language of fairy story as being 'green as wild celery', the wine 'red as blood', and the reader is teased with the possibility of the fairy-tale happy-ever-after ending which does not come about. Maryse Condé's story, which she calls a *'conte vrai'* (a true story), has a café in the post-war Latin Quarter as its backdrop, and provides the context for a reflection on the attitude of Parisians to visitors from the overseas territories, in this case Guadeloupe, and indeed the attitude of such visitors to the French capital and its occupants. In some of these texts the 'story' may be less important, but then the writer invents, muses, supposes, recalls, imagines, and the reverie is interspersed with narrative. Thus there may be stories within the *nouvelle*; for example, Colette's story of the mother and daughter in the Bois de Boulogne, or Butor's homely little snapshots or sketches of relationships in the conversations overheard at the Gare Saint-Lazare.

The premise for this collection is the undeniable rich-ness and variety in what has been written about Paris; different writers respond to different aspects of the city. I chose these texts mainly for how each reflects the character of a particular area, with the exception of the first and last. The first one, by Maupassant, leads us through the heart of Paris at night in a wandering nightmare, and the last, by Vincent Ravalec, takes place mainly in seedy areas out near the ring road, the *périphérique*. This reflects the way in which Paris, like most cities, has had to adapt and expand during the twentieth century, extending its communica-tions and its living space. There are twenty *arrondissements*, or administrative areas, in Paris; *quartier* denotes the smaller, more 'personal' locality. When Parisians refer to '*mon quartier*', they usually mean an area of a few streets and shops round where they live. In this volume the idea of the *quartier* is best expressed by Cyrille Fleischman's story about Jean Simpelberg, who never moves more than a street or two beyond the house he is living in, and for whom the other side of Paris is as remote as Timbuctoo. Fargue, in his *Les vingt arrondissements de Paris*, takes the administrative divisions in turn and invests each one with its own character and personality, a literary strategy which gives a structure and imaginative interest to his wanderings all over the capital, for which he was famous. I should point out that this volume does not imitate Fargue in that respect. The areas are not represented systematically, and I have not attempted to cover every area.

What struck me most particularly as I read and translated these texts was that many of them are concerned with the changing nature of the capital. When, in a town or city, buildings are knocked down or renovated, or new ones built, land is reallocated and redistributed to accommodate different contemporary needs. The construction of new roads and bridges and squares, the pedestrianization of streets, the planting or chopping-down of trees changes the character of that area, subtly or radically. Writers assimilate these changes and try to make sense of them for their readers and themselves. It is a theme that recurs frequently in these stories. People come and go, places remain. Or do they? In a great many of the stories we get a sense that

writers are fearful of places disappearing, and want to con-
serve, to record for posterity, the character of the street or
square or building, and simultaneously note or comment
on what is new. The Montmartre cemetery, or the Jardin du
Luxembourg, are instantly recognizable in the descriptions
of Colette and Condé, and if we visit them we can still find
the same features and atmosphere they have always had.
But one characteristic that many of these stories share is an
obsession with the passing of things, the changing city.
Major and irrevocable destruction and rebuilding took
place in Paris under Napoleon III who, with Haussmann in
the 1850s, razed to the ground many historic medieval
buildings and changed the face of the capital for ever.
Change sometimes provides the context for a story: for
example, what was happening in the Luxembourg area,
where Nerval was living in 1848, may have given him the
idea for his tale. More recently, the changes to the immediate architectural environment provide the backdrop for
Echenoz's story of the man obsessed with his wife's portrait
in an advertisement on the wall of a house that is being
demolished. Julien Green's reminiscence of Notre-Dame
pre- and post-war is also indirectly concerned with change,
though here in society rather than in the monument itself.

Miraculously, many areas in Paris still retain their own
special character, which survives, though sometimes only
just, the homogenization of the European city in the

twenty-first century. This is demonstrated quite clearly in some of the texts. The Rue du Commerce is vividly present when we read Réda's story, and the twentieth *arrondissement* is still recognizable in Léon-Paul Fargue's description. Colette's acerbic observations, written in 1913 about the cemetery in Montmartre, hold good today. The dead are still squashed beneath the Pont Caulaincourt, surrounded by picture palaces and the seamy trappings of tourist hotels and entertainments. In the Square des Batignolles described by Zola, you can still admire little rustic bridges, pools, and lawns; Arts et Métiers is still little more than a patch of enclosed gravel. The Château de Vauvert has long since disappeared, as Nerval tells us, only surviving in the phrase 'Va au diable Vauvert'; but the Passage de l'Enfer still occupies a mysterious corner off the Boulevard Raspail.

Old buildings and monuments in Paris, like those in many large European cities, are rich in their collective store of memories and associations. Public buildings like the Garnier Opéra, the Palais Royal, the Louvre, Notre-Dame, the Conciergerie, the Dome des Invalides carry with them through the centuries a weight of historical events. Streets, too, are rich in memories, and simply the name of a street like the Boulevard Saint-Michel, or the Champs-Élysées (for street names change only rarely) will bring to mind, depending on your generation, images of the riots of 1968, or the Liberation of Paris, or perhaps the Tour de France.

Métro stations in Paris are particularly resonant, since they are often named after famous battles, and are a constant reminder of the past: Réaumur-Sébastopol, Austerlitz, Iéna. Annie Saumont uses a historical event, the Battle of Jena, after which the métro station is named, to illustrate the feelings engendered by the breakdown in a relationship between a man and a woman.

For writers, and not just French ones, Paris has always held a unique fascination among European cities. The affection it inspires is global, and it would, of course, be possible to compile an anthology consisting of texts about Paris not originally written in French. Writers from Heine to Samuel Beckett have called it home. Here, however, we are just concerned with native French or Francophone writers. There is an enormous national literature on Paris; from Baudelaire to Prévert, Simone de Beauvoir to B. B. Dadié, a multitude of poets and novelists have written passionately and brilliantly about the city. But this volume contains only stories and short prose pieces. Maryse Condé from Guadeloupe, and Andrée Chedid from Egypt here represent French writing from overseas, bringing with them a new and valuable perspective.

The stories in this volume, though not in strict chrono-logical order, range from the mid-nineteenth century to the present day, and so to some extent they provide us with a historical perspective. Nerval's tale of the green monster was published in 1849, but goes back to a Paris at the beginning of the seventeenth century, a period he was especially fond of writing about. Maupassant's heroine belongs to turn-of-the-century Paris; Daeninckx's 1960s drop-out gives us an insight into the dramatic events of May 1968 when students' demonstrations all but brought down Charles de Gaulle's government. Ravalec's hero, who wins the lottery, is recognizably a man of the 1990s, and the 'plot' of Anna Gavalda's story turns on that plague or miracle of the twenty-first century, the mobile phone.

The city is viewed from many different standpoints. Its character emerges for each writer variously as glamorous, parochial, invasive, romantic, hostile, familiar. For Maupassant's heroine, an Emma Bovary-figure full of aspirations and romantic dreams, Paris is the thrilling capital, the city of sin, where she might finally realize those dreams, far away from the little provincial town where her husband is a rather unexciting lawyer; the storyteller's parents in *Portrait de famille* also glamorize the City of Light, which they have been deprived of during the years of the Second World War. For the characters in Ravalec's story—as in Daeninckx's, set in more recent times—the capital is a dangerous and hostile place, where those living on the edge of society often turn to crime. We see, too, how the capital looks through the eyes of a child, the little boy truanting from school who wanders round the area of the Champs-Élysées in Perec's story, as well as how Montparnasse appears to Fassola, a North African woman who gets the chance to return briefly from the world beyond and take a last look at the city she has loved so much. In Hugo Marsan's story a famous Paris park, the Parc Monceau, becomes significant in the life of a young invalid.

Some incidental sociological interest may derive from this anthology of stories about Paris. The pieces by Zola and Colette, for instance—writers' observations on two kinds of public place—are typically satirical and critical. Colette, originally from Burgundy, but who lived much of her life in Paris and died in her flat in the Palais Royal, is represented here by two pieces, on Montmartre cemetery and the Bois de Boulogne. Zola's ironic *Les Squares* is in some ways rather similar. He, too, is critical of the typical Parisian city-dweller who, while afraid of the real countryside, yet needs his square, his patch of grass, to provide some relief from the monstrous grey city he inhabits. There was also without doubt a critical intent in the writing of Nerval's story, since it was first published in a satirical magazine, with a sketch of a sergeant preparing to descend and attack with a band of soldiers. In 1849 it was reported that continuous raids were being made by the Paris police to root out supposed Monarchist plots. The story, though purporting to take place in the seventeenth century, is firmly rooted in the political events of nineteenth-century Paris.

However, I have not chosen these texts primarily for their social or historical interest, but because they evoke particular places. Paris gets ever closer to us, by air or rail, and for many visitors its attraction is not limited to the Eiffel Tower. These stories are worth reading because they are well written, by writers some of whom may be very familiar and others unfamiliar to English readers. All are worth knowing for the fresh insights they give us into different aspects of the capital.

A map has been included to help locate each story. Readers might have fun tracking down the locations; in so doing, they will add to their appreciation of the varied nature of this exceptional city.

Nightmare

Guy de Maupassant

I love the night passionately. I love it as I love my country, or my mistress, with an instinctive, deep, and unshakeable love. I love it with all my senses: I love to see it, I love to breathe it in, I love to open my ears to its silence, I love my whole body to be caressed by its blackness. Skylarks sing in the sunshine, the blue sky, the warm air, in the fresh morning light. The owl flies by night, a dark shadow passing through the darkness; he hoots his sinister, quivering hoot, as though he delights in the intoxicating black immensity of space.

The day exhausts me, irritates me. It is brutal, noisy. I struggle to get out of bed, I dress wearily and, against my inclination, I go out. I find each step, each movement, each gesture, each word, each thought as tiring as if I were lifting a crushing weight.

But when the sun goes down I feel strangely happy, my entire body fills with happiness. I wake up, I spring into life. As the shadows lengthen I feel quite different: younger, stronger, more alert, more contented. I watch the great soft darkness fall from the heavens and become denser. It swamps the city like a great wave that I cannot seize nor fathom, covering, blotting out, destroying colours and shapes, and enfolding houses, buildings, and living things in a silent embrace.

And then I want to hoot with pleasure like the owl, run over the roofs like a cat; and in my veins I feel the warmth of a sudden and irresistible desire for love.

I go, I walk, sometimes in darkened streets, sometimes in the woods near Paris, where I hear my sisters, the animals, and my brothers, the poachers, prowling.

Whatever you love passionately always destroys you in the end. But how can I explain what has happened to me? How can I make anyone even understand that I can write about it? I don't know, I don't know any more; all I know is that it is so.

So yesterday—was it yesterday?—yes, I'm sure it was, unless it was before that, another day, another month, another year—I don't know. But it must be yesterday, since the day has not begun, the sun has not reappeared. How long has the night lasted? How long? Who knows? Who will ever know?

So yesterday I went out after dinner, as I do every day. It was a lovely evening, very mild and warm. As I went down towards the boulevards I was looking up at the black sky above me, etched out by the roofs of the street, like a river with a rolling stream of undulating, heavenly bodies flowing through it, just like a real river.

In the evening air everything, from the planets down to the gas lamps, was brightly lit. So many lights were shining in the sky and in the town that they seemed to illuminate the shadows. Bright nights delight me more than long days of sunshine.

On the boulevards the cafés blazed with light; people were laughing, going in and out, having a drink. I went into the theatre for a moment or two. Which theatre? I have no idea. It was so dazzling in there that I found it depressing, and came out again somewhat cast down by the violent shock of the lights on the gold of the balcony, and the artificial sparkle of the enormous crystal chandelier, the lights leading down to the pit, and that harsh, false glare. I reached the Champs-Élysées, where the cafés-concerts seemed to be burning like so many fires among the green leaves. The flecks of yellow light on the chestnut trees made them look painted; they looked like phosphorescent trees. And the electric globes, just like pale but brilliant moons, like moon eggs fallen out of the sky, like monstrous living pearls, made the dirty, ugly gas filaments and the strings of coloured glass pale beneath their mysterious, royal, mother-of-pearl brightness.

I stopped under the Arc de Triomphe to look at the avenue, the long, wonderful starry avenue leading into Paris between its two rows of lights, and the stars! The stars in the sky; unknown stars flung out here there and everywhere into the vastness of space, drawing their crazy patterns that fill a man with dreams and wonderment.

I went into the Bois de Boulogne and stayed there a very long time. A peculiar trembling had seized hold of me, an unexpectedly powerful emotion, a mental exaltation bordering on madness.

I walked for a long long time. And then I retraced my steps.

What time was it when I passed beneath the Arc de Triomphe once more? I don't know. The city was falling asleep and large black clouds were gradually spreading out across the sky.

For the first time I had the feeling that something novel and untoward was about to happen. It seemed to me that it was cold, that the air was getting denser, that the night, my beloved night, was weighing heavy upon my heart. The avenue now was deserted, except for two policemen walking along near the rank where the cabs were drawn up, and on the cobbles, only faintly lit by the dying gas lamps, a row of vegetable carts on their way to Les Halles. They were driving slowly, loaded with carrots, turnips, and cabbages. The drivers were asleep and invisible, the horses walked with an uneven tread, silently following the cart in front on the cobbles. As they passed under each pavement light, the carrots glowed red, the turnips white, and the cabbages green. And one after another, these carts, red as fire, white as silver, green as emerald, moved along the road. I followed them, then turned into the Rue Royale and came back along the boulevards. There was no one there, no lights in the cafés, just a few laggards hurrying home. I had never seen Paris so dead, so deserted. I took out my pocket watch. It was two o'clock.

A powerful urge impelled me forward, a need to walk. So I went as far as the Bastille. There I realized I had never before seen such a dark night, for I could not even make out the July column; its golden spirit was lost in the unfathomable darkness. A dome of cloud, thick as space itself, had obscured the stars and seemed to be descending to reduce the earth to nothing.

I went back again. There was no longer anybody around. However, at the Place du Château d'Eau a drunk almost bumped into me, and then disappeared. I could hear his noisy, uneven step for quite some time. I walked on. Level with the Faubourg Montmartre a cab went by, on its way down to the Seine. I hailed it. The coachman did not answer. A woman was lurking near the Rue Drouot: 'Listen, sir.' I hurried on to avoid the hand held out to me. Then, nothing. Outside the Vaudeville a rag-and-bone man was searching along the gutter. His little lantern floated just above the ground. I asked him: 'What time is it, my good fellow?'

He muttered: 'How do I know? Haven't got a watch.'

Then I suddenly realized that the gaslights were all out. I know they put them out early, before dawn, at this time of year, to save money. But the day was still a long way off, such a long way from dawning!

Let's go to Les Halles, I thought. At least I shall find a bit of life there.

I set off, but could not even see enough to tell which direction I should take. Slowly I made my way forward, as you do in a wood, identifying the roads by counting.

In front of the Crédit Lyonnais, a dog growled. I turned down the Rue de Grammont, and got lost. I wandered round for a while then recognized the Bourse by the iron railings surrounding it. The whole of Paris was sleeping, in a deep, terrifying sleep. But some way off a cab was driving along, just one cab, perhaps the one which had passed in front of me a little while ago. I tried to reach it, going towards the noise of its wheels, through the dark, deserted streets; dark, dark, dark, like death.

I lost my way again. Where was I? How foolish they were to put out the lights so early! Not a single passer-by, not one late homegoer, not a solitary prowler, not one cat yowling for his mate. Nothing.

So where were the night watchmen? I said to myself: I'll shout and they'll come. I shouted. Nobody answered.

I shouted louder. My voice faded, without an echo, weak, stifled, crushed by the night, by the impenetrable night.

I screamed: 'Help! Help! Help!'

My desperate cries remained unanswered. So what time was it, then? I took out my pocket watch, but didn't have a light. I listened to the faint tick of the little mechanism with unwonted delight. It seemed to be alive. I was not so alone. How odd! I set off again like a blind man, feeling for the walls with my stick, and every moment I raised my eyes to heaven, hoping for daybreak. But the sky was black, quite black, more deeply black than the town.

What time could it possibly be? I had been walking, or so it seemed, for ever. My legs were giving way beneath me, my breast was heaving, and I was dreadfully hungry.

I decided to ring at the first *porte-cochère*.[1] I pulled on the brass bell and the noise sounded through the echoing house. The noise it made was odd, as though this vibration were the only noise in the house.

---

[1] A carriage entrance leading into a courtyard.

I waited, there was no reply; no one came to open the door. Again I rang. Again I waited. Nothing!

I was terrified! I ran to the next house, and rang the bell twenty times in the dark passageway where the concierge must have been asleep. But he did not wake, and I went on further, pulling the rings or the knobs as hard as I could, pushing, kicking, and beating with my stick at the obstinately closed doors.

And suddenly I realized I was reaching Les Halles. Les Halles were deserted, not a sound, not a movement, not a cart, not a man, not a bunch of vegetables or flowers. It was empty, motionless, abandoned, dead.

I was seized with a terrible dread. What was happening? Oh God, what was happening?

I set off again. But the time? What about the time? Who could tell me the time? No clock was ringing in the steeples or in the buildings. I thought: I shall open the glass on my watch and feel the hands with my fingers. I took out my watch; it was no longer working, it had stopped. Nothing at all, not a whisper in the town, not one gleam of light, not the faintest rustle. Nothing! Nothing! Not even the far-off wheels of a cab, nothing!

I was down by the river, from which rose an icy chill.

Was the Seine still flowing?

I had to know, I found the steps, I went down, I couldn't hear the current flowing under the arches of the bridge . . . .

Still more steps . . . then sand . . . mud . . . then the water. I put in my arm . . . the river was flowing it was flowing . . . cold . . . cold . . . cold . . . almost frozen . . . almost dried up . . . almost dead.

And I knew I should never have the strength to go up again . . . and that I too was going to die there . . . of hunger—of exhaustion—and of cold.

The Green Monster

Gérard de Nerval

I. The Devil's Castle

Let me tell you the tale of one of the oldest inhabitants of Paris. He used to be called 'the devil Vauvert'.

That is the origin of the expression: 'It's the devil Vauvert!' or 'Go to the devil Vauvert!'

It mean: Go . . . take a walk down the Champs-Élysées!

Carters often say, when they mean something is a long way off: 'It's at the devil Vauvert's!'

In other words, you are going to have to pay through the nose for the job you are asking them to do. However, this is an incorrect and corrupt usage, like several other Parisian expressions.

The devil of Vauvert is quintessentially Parisian. If we

are to believe the historians, he has been living in Paris for hundreds of years. Saural,[1] Félibien, Sainte-Foix, and Dulaure[2] have all told lengthy anecdotes about him.

It seems that he lived first of all in the castle of Vauvert, which was situated in the place where the jolly Chartreuse ball is now held, at the far end of the Luxembourg, opposite the tree-lined walks of the Observatoire in the Rue d'Enfer.[3]

This castle, which was of ill repute, was partly demolished, and the ruins became a dependency of the Charterhouse monastery where Jean de la Lune, the nephew of the anti-pope Benedict XIII, died in 1414. Jean de la Lune had been suspected of having dealings with a certain devil, who was possibly the familiar spirit of the old castle, for it is common knowledge that every feudal establishment possessed one of these.

The historians have not passed on any details of this fascinating period.

The devil of Vauvert was much talked about again at the time of Louis XIII. For quite some time, a loud noise had

---

[1] Nerval perhaps means Jacques Saurin, a famous Protestant preacher (1677–1730).

[2] French historians: Michel Félibien (1666–1719), Jacques-Antoine Dulaure (1755–1835), Germain-François Poullain de Sainte-Foix (1698–1776).

[3] There was formerly a Rue d'Enfer, which ran along the edge of what is now the Luxembourg Gardens. A 'Passage d'Enfer' exists off the Boulevard Raspail. Before 1887, Boulevard Raspail was called the Boulevard d'Enfer.

been heard each evening coming from a house built out of the remains of the former monastery. The owners had been absent for several years.

The neighbours were frightened out of their wits. They went to tell the lieutenant of police, who sent out men with bows and arrows.

Imagine these soldiers' amazement when they heard a medley of raucous laughter and the clinking of glasses. At first they thought it was coiners having an orgy, and since, judging by the volume, there seemed to be a large number, they went to fetch reinforcements.

But the force was still felt to be insufficient. Not one sergeant was anxious to lead his men into this building, where the din sounded like that of a whole army.

Towards morning, finally enough troops arrived, and they entered the house. They found nothing.

The darkness had vanished and the sun was shining.

They searched all day and then decided that the noise must be coming up from the catacombs, known to be situated underneath this area.

They prepared to go in. But by the time the police had taken up their positions it was nightfall again, and the noise began again, worse than ever.

This time nobody dared go back down because it was quite clear that there was nothing but bottles in the cellar and that it must be the devil making them dance.

They contented themselves with occupying the approach roads to the castle and with asking the clergy to pray for them.

The priests offered up quantities of prayers and they even sent along holy water to sprinkle through a window in the basement.

The noise still persisted.

II. The Sergeant

For a whole week the approaches to the area were packed with crowds of terrified Parisians demanding news.

Finally a sergeant from the marshal's house, who was bolder than the rest, offered to go into the haunted cellar on condition he received a sum of money, which was to be paid, in the event of his demise, to a dressmaker by the name of Margot.

He was a worthy man, by nature more amorous than credulous. Hs adored this dressmaker, who, as well as being good at housekeeping, was also very smart. She might almost be said to be a bit close with her money; she had not the slightest intention of marrying a mere sergeant with no fortune.

But when the sergeant was given the money, he became a new man.

At the prospect now before him, he shouted that he believed neither in God nor the devil and that he would get to the bottom of the noise.

'What do you believe in then?' one of his companions asked.

'I believe,' he replied, 'in the Lieutenant of Crime and the Provost of Paris.'

That was going a bit too far.

He put his sword beneath his teeth, took a pistol in each hand, and set off down the steps.

As he reached the cellar floor, the most extraordinary spectacle met his eyes.

All the bottles were dancing, and executing the most graceful figures of a wild sarabande.

The ones with green seals were male and the ones with red were female.

There was even a band installed upon the wooden planks where the bottles were kept.

The empty bottles fluted like wind instruments, the broken ones clashed like cymbals, and the cracked bottles made a shrill, penetrating sound, rather like violins.

The sergeant had had a glass or two before undertaking this expedition and, feeling extremely relieved by the sight of nothing but bottles, he, too, started to dance.

Then, made more and more bold by this gay and charming spectacle, he picked up a beautiful bottle with a long neck, a pale Bordeaux it seemed, elegantly sealed in red, and pressed it amorously to his breast.

There was frenzied laughter throughout the cellar. The

sergeant, much intrigued, let the bottle drop and it smashed into a thousand pieces.

The dancing stopped, cries of fear could be heard from every corner of the cellar, and the sergeant felt his hair stand on end as he watched the spilt wine turn into a pool of blood before his very eyes.

The body of a naked woman, her blonde hair soaked in the wet blood, was lying spread out on the floor at his feet.

Had it been the devil himself the sergeant would not have been so terrified, but this sight filled him with horror. He remembered that he was supposed to give some account of what he had been sent out to do and, grabbing a green sealed bottle which seemed to be leering at him contemptuously, he shouted: 'At least I'll get one of you!'

The only reply was a roar of laughter.

He had got back to the steps, however, and, waving the bottle at his friends, he shouted: 'Here's the little devil! What a lot of chickens you are—and he used another more colourful word—too scared to go down there.'

His was a bitter irony. The archers rushed down to the cellar and found nothing but a broken bottle of Bordeaux. Everything else was in its place.

The archers lamented the fate of the broken bottle; but now they were emboldened and they each wanted to take a bottle up with them.

They were given leave to drink them.

The sergeant from the marshal's house said: 'I shall keep mine for my wedding day.'

They could not refuse to give him the promised sum of money, he married the dressmaker and . . .

You are thinking that they had a lot of children? They had only one.

III. What Happened Afterwards

On the sergeant's wedding day, which took place at the Rapée, he put the infamous bottle with the green seal in between himself and his wife and shared the wine out carefully between the two of them.

The bottle was as green as the wild celery, and the wine was red as blood.

Nine months later the dressmaker gave birth to a little green monster with red horns on its forehead.

So begone all ye maidens, and dance at the Charterhouse . . . on the site of the castle of Vauvert!

Meanwhile the child grew in stature, if not in goodness.

Two things worried his parents: his green colour, and a caudal appendix, which at first seemed just an elongated coccyx, but which slowly took on the appearance of a veritable tail.

They went to consult physicians, who declared they could not possibly cut it out without putting the child's life in danger. They added that it was rather a rare case, but that examples could be found in the works of Herodotus and Pliny the Younger. The Fourier system was not yet in use.[4]

As for the colour, it was blamed on a predominance of the bilious humour. Several caustic treatments were tried out, to soften the violent hue of the epidermis and, after a great number of lotions and frictions, they managed to reduce it to first bottle-green, then viridian, then apple-green. At one point the skin appeared to have become completely white, but by evening it reverted to its usual tone.

The sergeant and the dressmaker could not get over the sorrow brought upon them by this little monster, who was becoming ever more obstinate, bad-tempered, and mischievous.

Their depression drove them to indulge in a vice only too common in people of their sort. They took to drink.

But the sergeant only ever wanted to drink wine from bottles with red seals, and his wife only from green.

Every time the sergeant was in a drunken stupor he saw in his dreams the woman covered in blood, whose apparition had terrified him in the cellar after he had smashed the bottle.

The woman was saying to him: 'Why did you clasp me to

---

[4] François-Marie-Charles Fourier (1772–1835) was a social philosopher who suggested that Nature would in future produce different forms of human life. These 'monsters', presumably like Nerval's green monster, would be put to use in the new order of humanity.

your heart, and then destroy me . . . when I loved you so much?'

Each time the sergeant's wife had drunk rather too much from the green sealed ones, a huge and terrible devil would appear to her while she slept, saying: 'Why are you so surprised to see me . . . when you have drunk from the bottle? Am I not the father of your child?'

What a mystery!

On reaching the age of thirteen, the child vanished.

His distraught parents carried on drinking, but never again did those dreadful apparitions come to torment their sleep.

IV. The Moral

So that is how the sergeant was punished for his lack of piety—and the dressmaker for her greed.

V.

What became of the green monster?

Nobody ever found out.

The Last Napoleon[1]

Honoré de Balzac

One afternoon in Paris at about three o'clock, a young man went down some steps into the gardens of the Palais Royal. He walked slowly beneath the yellow, sickly-looking lime trees in the north *allée*, sometimes raising his head to stare at the windows of the gaming parlours. But it seemed as if it were not yet time for the fateful doors of these silent halls to open, for all that he could see, through the panes of glass, were employees standing idly around, their faces all cast in the same ignoble and sinister mould, like larvae[2] waiting for

---

[1] A napoleon, sometimes called a louis, was a gold coin in use until the First World War.

[2] A larva in Roman mythology was an evil spirit who had committed a crime or suffered a violent death.

their prey. So, with a melancholic gesture, the young man shifted his gaze back to the ground again.

His listless walk brought him to a fountain, whose graceful showers were at that moment being lit up in the sunshine, but he went round, not stopping to admire the colourful play of light, nor even looking at the thousand facets of the water shimmering in the artificial pool. His entire body betrayed a deep indifference to the things around him; a bitter, disdainful smile made little lines in the corners of his mouth. His cold, ironic expression, which was such a noticeable characteristic, was rendered even more distressing by his tender years; a strange anomaly in a bright face glowing with life, dazzlingly pure, the face of a twenty-five year old. That head drew your attention. A mysterious spirit dwelt on his pale brow. His head was thin and delicately formed, his hair fine and fair. Although his eyes betrayed his sickness or sorrow, they were uncommonly bright and lustrous.

Seeing this young man, poets would have imagined long hours of study, nights spent by the light of a studious lamp; doctors, noticing the redness of the cheeks, the yellow circles around the eyes, the rapidity of the breathing, would have suspected some heart or lung condition. Observers would have admired him. The uncaring would have trodden on his toes . . . . This mysterious young man was neither well- nor ill-attired, his clothes did not lead one to believe he was a man favoured by fortune; but in order to discover the secret of this deep misery, one would have needed the wisdom of a physiologist, who would be able to guess why the cloak had been so carefully done up!

The young man went to lean against the iron railings surrounding the flowerbeds, crossed his arms on his chest, and gazed sadly, but resignedly, at the buildings, the fountain, and the passers-by. That look of abandonment told of many a failure, of much disappointment; but in the tense way he held himself, there was, too, an enormous amount of courage. The impassive expression of one who is suicidal dominated his face. None of life's curiosities tempted this soul any more. He was both agitated and calm.

Suddenly a shudder went through him . . . . He had heard, as by some prerogative of the damned, the ringing of the bell, the opening of the doors, the clattering on the stairways . . . . He looked up at the windows of the gaming parlours. Men's heads were moving back and forth in the rooms . . . .

He pulled himself together and calmly set off walking. It was with some determination that he turned into the *allée*, climbed the steps, went through the door, and found himself in front of the baize table, perhaps rather sooner than he would have wished; but a brave soul likes to settle things quickly.

It was not a huge gathering. There were a few hoary old men sitting around a table, but many chairs remained unoccupied. The one or two strangers—who were apparently from the South, to judge by their faces, blazing with desperation and greed—contrasted starkly with these old hands, who were well used to the suffering of the gaming room; they seemed like old convicts no longer fearful of the galley.

The motionless 'croupier' and the 'banker' surveyed the players with a mortal indifference . . . the minions strolled nonchalantly around. Seven or eight people had ranged themselves around the table, to witness in the faces of the players, and the moving of the gold coins, how the lots would fall. They were there, without anything else to do, silently watching . . . . They came into this room in the same way as the common people go to the Place de la Grève.[3] They exchanged glances when the young man, without sitting down, took up his position in front of a chair.

'Place your bets!' cried a shrill voice.

Each player did so.

The young man threw on to the cloth a gold coin he had in his hand, and his blazing eyes travelled first from the cards to the coin and then from the coin to the cards. During this brief moment, those looking on could not perceive

---

[3] Now the Place de l'Hotel de Ville, it was the square where executions took place until the Revolution.

the slightest sign of emotion upon his cold, resigned face, when the most violent conflict known to man was tormenting him. All that happened was that the stranger closed his eyes when he had lost, and his lips went ashen. But presently he raised his eyelids, his lips took on their coral hue again. He watched the rake seize hold of his last piece of gold, assumed an expression of total indifference, and then vanished without looking for the slightest sign of compassion in the frozen faces of those around him.

He went down the steps whistling '*Di tanti palpiti*'[4] so softly, so quietly, that perhaps he was the only one who could hear the notes. Then, slowly, hesitatingly, he made his way towards the Tuileries, seeing neither houses, nor passers-by, but walking as if in the middle of the desert, hearing only one voice—the voice of Death; a lost soul, brooding and bewildered, where there was one thought, and one alone . . . .

He crossed the Tuileries gardens, taking the short cut to get to the Pont Royal. Then he came to a halt at a point over the centre of the middle arch, and his gaze plunged deep into the waters of the Seine.

---

4 A well-known aria from Rossini's opera *Tancredi*.

SQUARE
René VIVIANI
(1863 - 1925)

Squares

Émile Zola

In the next few days the gates of the new Parmentier Square, built on the land of the old Popincourt abattoirs, will be opened to the public. Now and again Paris, blinded by dust, drops a small island of greenery like this into its sea of grey houses. Along come gardeners with barrow-loads of clods and clumps of turf. They bring trees and rocks; a pond is dug, paths are laid out, and pots of flowers are sunk into the soil along the edges. And hey presto, a week later, there is a little garden all ready for people to walk in, exactly as if it has been stuck there by the scene-shifters from the Opéra Comique.

In small provincial towns the grass grows thick between the paving stones; some little streets asleep in their green shade look like those unassuming paths that skirt the edge of woods, and you are in the midst of the countryside, its hills and forests stretched out along the horizon. But in Paris the pavements are scorched and discoloured by the tread of many feet. The streets are great dusty highways, like railway tracks, and not a scrap of moss to be seen. So Paris is obliged to create a lawn for her own use, a splendid, clean, civilized lawn. And where roads meet, they cultivate patches of grass so that the inhabitants, who otherwise would have to travel miles before seeing a single blade, are spared the trouble of making real journeys.

At certain times of day, in certain seasons, the Parisian feels the need for Nature, but it is a Nature tailored to his needs, easy on the eye, gift-wrapped, painted, and varnished; the kind that can be enclosed on four sides by rows of houses. Out in the countryside under the wide open skies he would be worried, nervous of the vast horizons.

Those who live in the faubourg—the manual workers, the shop assistants, the *rentiers*—don't care to venture out to the woods in the suburbs. They stop at the moats by the fortifications. They feel comfortable on the banks planted with sickly-looking trees, on the faded yellow grass. They spread out their handkerchiefs and sit on them, turning their backs to the countryside and looking at the noisy, smoking monster of a city stretched out before their eyes.

In the centre of Paris, the poets, the retired captains, the young women, and the nurses go and sit on the chairs in the Tuileries, the Luxembourg, or the Jardin des Plantes. Each park has its regulars, those who make a point of visiting it, as though it were their duty. They do not notice the trees or the flowerbeds. They seem to be under the impression that the trees are made of tin and the flowers just come out of a hat shop. They go on believing this quite happily.

The square, which is like a miniature park, is adequate for these good people. If they did not have squares they would be content with a pot of grass at home. But Paris humours them by nailing down carpets of greenery in their public places. The people of Paris shall have their grass!

It must be said that some squares are nothing more than wide pavements with trees. The one at Arts et Métiers, for example, has more gravel than grass, and the mangy patches of green under the Tour Saint Jacques are hardly sufficient to provide one dinner for a flock of sheep.

Other squares put you in mind of an English garden. The ones just opened next to the new Temple and behind the Église des Batignolles are greatly coveted by retired milliners, who dream of planting similar ones around their villas at Asnières. In these squares, beds of flowers are laid out with great artistry to delight the eye, the yellow sandy paths bordered by green lawns; streams are overhung by lovely little rustic bridges; there are waterfalls, and tiered pools where pierrots come to dip their toes. Only the noise of cabs disturbs the shady calm of this verdure. A railing runs all the way round it. It looks like a small piece of Nature which has been locked up for misbehaving.

It is becoming the fashion to plant a few bushes outside churches. There are 'religious' squares where the statues they put up, supposedly of saints, grin at you like Pan from out of the shadows, and angels spread their innocent white wings like doves. So Trinity and Sainte-Clotilde—two disproportionately large children's playthings—have flowerbeds, the sweetness of whose blossoms and the shamelessness of whose insects must seriously trouble the pious as they emerge from divine service. Ladybirds copulate freely there upon the pure white lilies.

Squares everywhere! The future belongs to the gardener. Today we have something like twenty squares in Paris. Obviously there is not enough grass for the whole population, and my fondest hope is that in ten years' time every pavement will have its border of box.

Every time I sit on a bench in a square in sad contemplation of the well-kept, professionally designed lawns, the same memory comes back to me and fills me with a deep melancholy.

It was in a village by the Durance on a dreadfully hot afternoon in July. Beside the road there was a castle, built in the reign of Louis XV and now abandoned to the wind and the rain. There were cracks in it and it was going to rack and ruin. Through the holes where the windows had been you could see bits of white flaking off the ceilings on to the floors of the great empty rooms. Behind the castle was a sleepy little park.

I have never before or since seen such an abandoned place. It was like the verdant domain of the Sleeping Beauty. No gardener had entered there for nigh on a hundred years. Beneath the weeds you could hazard a guess as to how the garden had been laid out, with paths, ponds, lawns, and flights of steps. Cupids, broken and stripped of their charms, still smiled at you from the depths of the undergrowth. A shawl of moss covered the shoulders of a large Venus, shivering in a grotto. This little place had put on its beauty spots during the years of the Regency. All combed and curled, it must have been used for pasturing Florian's sheep.[1] Then Nature in her harsh fashion had come to cast the power of her springtimes over all this coquetterie in the boudoir. While the powdered nobility of the last reign were drowning in the blood of 1793, Nature's own revolution was taking place in this park, bringing about the triumph of democracy with its blades of grass and its oak trees.

---

[1] Zola is referring to the pastoral style popular during the Regency of 1715–22. 'Florian' is a name one might associate with a shepherd.

Now trees have grown up in the middle of the long walks. The garden has turned into forest, virgin forest, a black curtain of ivy and nightshade. Weeds have grown up as high as the branches. It is nothing now but a dark thicket cut through with occasional wells and shafts of light. The steps have come loose and wallflowers have sprung up in the cracks. Columns of white birches have grown in the mud-filled ponds. The carpet of moss reaches right up to the coping on the wall, suffocating all the throbbing life in the sap. And over to the left, in the depths of the garden, the only sound there is comes from a fountain dripping its cold clear water, drop by drop, into a cracked basin.

At two o'clock under a blazing sun it is good to forget your troubles in the cold freshness of this leafy place. I suppose if they shut the gates of the squares for a hundred years the rampant forces of Nature would do their work there as well. But gardeners would come and quickly get those rebellious weeds in order. They would fell the oaks, tear off the cloak of ivy and the carpet of moss and plant the sort of sanitized, velvety little lawn that all respectable, civilized gardens wear.

A Parisian Adventure

Guy de Maupassant

Do women feel anything more keenly than curiosity? No, they will go to any lengths to find out, to know, to feel, what they have always dreamed of! Once their excited curiosity has been aroused, women will stoop to anything, commit any folly, take any risks. They stop at nothing. I am speaking of women who are real women, who operate on three different levels. Superficially cool and rational, they have three secret compartments: the first is constantly full of womanly fret and anxiety; the second of a sort of innocent guile, like the fearsome sophistry of the self-righteous; and the last is filled with an engaging dishonesty, a charming deviousness, a consummate duplicity, with all those perverse qualities in fact that can drive a foolish, unwary lover to suicide, but which by others may be judged quite delightful.

The woman whose adventure I am going to relate was from the provinces and of good, if unremarkable character until then. Outwardly she led a quiet life in the home, dividing her time between a very busy husband, and two children whom she brought up in an exemplary fashion. In her heart, however, there simmered an unsatisfied curiosity, and she craved the unknown. She was forever dreaming of Paris, and she read the society pages avidly. The reports of society dinners, fashion, and high life made her seethe with longing. But what disturbed her oddly, more than anything else, were the hints and innuendoes, the clever words that pulled the veil up just a little to let her glimpse the sinful passions and pleasures on the distant horizon.

Living where she did, she viewed Paris as the apotheosis of glorious luxury and vice.

During the long nights, lulled by the regular snoring of her husband asleep on his back beside her, his neckerchief tied round his head, she thought about the famous men whose names shone out from the front covers of newspapers like bright stars in a dark sky. She ascribed to them exciting lives of constant debauchery, orgies of terrifying voluptuousness, like those in ancient times, refinements of sensuality of such complexity she could not even begin to conceive of them.

The boulevards seemed to her an abyss of human passions. She was certain that extraordinary love affairs were being conducted in the houses there. At the same time she felt herself getting older; she was growing old without knowing anything of life except those detested, monotonous chores that make for domestic happiness—or so they say. She was still pretty. Her sheltered life had preserved her like a fruit over-wintering in a store-cupboard; but she was consumed, harrowed, overwhelmed by her secret longings. She wondered if she would die without ever experiencing the throes of passion, without ever once, just once, plunging into the sea of sensual pleasure that was Paris.

With great perseverance she made preparations for a journey to Paris. She invented an excuse, got herself invited by relatives, and set off on her own, since her husband was unable to accompany her.

As soon as she arrived she dreamed up reasons that would allow her to go off by herself for a couple of days, or rather nights, if necessary. She had discovered friends, she told them, who lived just outside Paris, in the country.

Then she began searching. She walked up and down the boulevards without seeing anything apart from the numbered street-walkers.[1] She scrutinized the big cafés and read the personal columns in *Le Figaro*, which every

---

[1] Prostitutes at the time usually had to wear numbers for identification purposes.

morning seemed to her like a warning signal, love's reminder to her.

But nothing occurred to put her on the track of those great orgies of artists and actresses. Nothing revealed to her the temples of debauchery she imagined could only be unlocked by one magic word, like the cave in the *Thousand and One Nights*, or the catacombs in Rome, where the rituals of a persecuted religion were practised in secrecy.

Her relatives, from the lower-middle classes, were not in a position to introduce her to any of the prominent men whose names buzzed round and round in her head. In despair, she was beginning to think about returning home when she had a piece of good fortune.

One day, as she was going down the Rue de la Chaussée d'Antin, she stopped to look at a shop full of those Japanese curios that are so brightly coloured you feel cheered by the very sight of them. She was studying the funny little ivories, the large burnished oriental vases, and the strange bronzes, when she overheard the proprietor inside the shop very respectfully showing a large pot-bellied grotesque to a bald-headed little man with a grey stubble. He said there was only one of its kind.

At every sentence the shopkeeper uttered, the collector's name, which was very famous, rang out like a clarion call. The other customers, young women and well-dressed gentlemen, darted swift, discreet, polite glances at the famous writer, who, for his part, was contemplating the porcelain figure with a keen interest. They were one as ugly as the other, like two ugly brothers issued from the same womb.

The shopkeeper was saying: 'I'll let it go to you, Monsieur Jean Varin, for a thousand francs, exactly what I gave for it. To anyone else it would be fifteen hundred, but I want to keep my artistic clientele, so I offer them a special price. They all come to me, Monsieur Jean Varin. Monsieur Busnach bought a large antique goblet from me only yesterday. The other day I sold a pair of candlesticks like that— lovely, are they not?—to Monsieur Alexandre Dumas. If Monsieur Zola saw that piece you're holding there it would be sold, Monsieur Varin.'

The writer hesitated, quite unable to decide. He was attracted by the object but was thinking about the price, and took no more notice of the interested glances than if he had been alone in the desert.

She had gone in trembling, eyes fixed boldly upon him, never stopping to consider his age or whether he was good-looking or well-dressed. It was Jean Varin himself, Jean Varin!

After a long struggle, after some painful hesitation, he put the piece back on the table. 'No, it's too dear,' he said.

The shopkeeper waxed more eloquent still. 'Oh, Monsieur Varin, too dear? Why it's worth two thousand francs if it's worth a cent.'

The man of letters, still looking at the little man with the enamelled eyes, replied sadly: 'I'm sure you're right, but it's too dear for me.'

In a sudden fit of boldness she came forward: 'How much would I have to pay for the little man?'

Taken aback, the shopkeeper replied: 'Fifteen hundred francs, Madame.'

'I'll take it.'

The writer, who had not even noticed her till then, swung round quickly and looked her up and down, observing her out of half-closed eyes. Then he took in the details of her appearance like the connoisseur he was.

She was attractive, vivacious, suddenly alive with the flame which had been dormant in her until now. After all, a woman who buys a curio for 1,500 francs is not just anybody.

At that moment she made a gesture full of charm and delicacy. Turning to him she said in an unsteady voice: 'I'm so sorry, Monsieur, no doubt I have been rather hasty. Perhaps you had not finished making up your mind.'

He bowed. 'Indeed I had, Madame.'

But she pressed on, in a flurry of emotion. 'Well, Monsieur, if you should see fit to change your mind today or later, the curio is yours. I only bought it because you liked it.'

He smiled, evidently flattered. 'How did you know who I am?' he asked.

She spoke of her admiration for him, mentioned some of his books, became eloquent.

He had leaned against a piece of furniture in order to chat to her and, levelling his sharp gaze upon her, he tried to make her out.

The shopkeeper, who was only too pleased to have such living publicity with new customers coming in, called out now and again from the far side of the shop, 'Hey, look at this Monsieur Jean Varin, what do you think of this?' And then every head would go up and a shiver of pleasure went through her at being seen chatting with one of the Greats in this intimate fashion.

Intoxicated by her success she was filled with the supreme audacity of a general who is about to make an assault. 'Monsieur, do me the very great honour of accepting this ornament to remind you of a woman who greatly admires you and who has spent ten minutes in your company.'

He refused. She insisted. He resisted, enjoying himself hugely and laughing out loud.

She stood her ground. 'All right, I shall take it to your house immediately. Where do you live?'

He refused to give her his address, but she found out by asking the man in the shop, and when she had paid for her new acquisition, she ran off in the direction of a cab. The writer ran to catch her up, not wanting to put himself in the compromising position of receiving a present and not knowing who to thank for it. Just as she was jumping into the carriage, he reached her and leaped in, sprawling across her, almost falling on top of her as he was thrown off-balance by the cab moving off. Much discomfited, he sat down beside her.

He begged and pleaded with her, but she was not to be persuaded. As they arrived outside his door she set out her conditions. If you fulfil all my wishes today, I will agree not to give you this. He thought the notion so droll, he agreed.

'What do you normally do at this time of day?' she asked him.

After a brief hesitation he said, 'I go for a walk.'

In a resolute voice she commanded: 'To the Bois!' and they set off.

She made him tell her the names of all the famous women, especially the not-so-virtuous ones, and relate the intimate details of their private lives, habits, homes, vices.

Evening came. 'What do you usually do at this time of day?' she asked.

'I take a glass of absinthe,' he laughed.

Gravely she replied: 'Let us go and drink absinthe.'

They went into a large café on the boulevard where he was often seen, and he met up with some of his fellow writers. He introduced them all. She was exultant. And the words 'at last, at last' were echoing through her brain.

Time passed. She asked: 'Is this the time you usually have dinner?'

'Yes, Madame,' he answered.

'Then let us have dinner, Monsieur.'

As they left the Café Bignon she asked him. 'What do you do in the evenings?'

He looked hard at her. 'It depends. Sometimes I go to the theatre.'

'Then let us go to the theatre.'

They had free tickets for a revue because of him, and, the crowning glory, she was seen by the whole of the auditorium sitting next to him in the dress circle.

After the performance he gallantly kissed her hand. 'It only remains for me to thank you, Madame, for a most delightful day.' She cut him short. 'What do you do each night at this time?'

'Well—I go home.'

She started to laugh in a trembling sort of way.

'Then let us go home, Monsieur.'

No more words were exchanged. Now and again a spasm shook her from head to toe, for she wanted to run away and she wanted to stay, but in her heart she knew for certain she wanted to carry this thing through to its conclusion.

As they climbed the stairs she clung to the banisters, her feelings threatening to overwhelm her. He went up first, out of breath, carrying a lighted taper.

As soon as she was in the bedroom she undressed quickly and slipped into bed without a word, nestling up against the wall, waiting.

She was uncomplicated, as well might be the wedded wife of a country lawyer, but he was more demanding than a pasha with three tails. They did not understand one another, not in the slightest.

Then he went to sleep. The night passed, disturbed only by the ticking of the clock. As she lay there unmoving she turned over in her mind her nights of conjugal love. In the yellow light of the Chinese lantern she looked in despair at the little fat man lying beside her, his distended belly making the sheet swell like a gas balloon. He was snoring noisily like an organ pipe, with long-drawn-out intakes of breath and funny choking noises. As he slept, his few remaining hairs were brushed up in an odd fashion, as if tired of remaining so long in their fixed position upon the poor bald pate that they were intended to cover up. From out of the corner of his half-open mouth ran a trickle of saliva.

Dawn came at last and a little daylight filtered through the drawn curtains. She rose and dressed without a sound and had already half-opened the door when the noise of the key in the lock woke him and he rubbed his eyes.

He remained thus for a few seconds before becoming fully conscious. Then, when he remembered the whole adventure, he asked: 'So, you're off, are you?'

She stood there feeling very embarrassed. 'Yes, it's morning,' she stammered.

He sat up in bed. 'This time it's my turn to ask you something.'

There was no reply, so he continued: 'You have astonished me no end since yesterday. Now tell me honestly why you have done all this. I don't understand it at all.'

She went over to him quietly, blushing like a virgin. 'I wanted to know what . . . vice was like, and . . . well, it's not much fun.'

She fled downstairs and ran out into the street.

The army of street-sweepers were cleaning up. They were sweeping the pavements, the cobbles, pushing all the rubbish into the gutter. With the same rhythmical motion, like that of the reapers in the fields, they swept the piles of dirt in front of them into semicircles. She saw them in every street she went down, working automatically in the same way, like puppets.

And she felt that something in her, her excited dreams, had also just been swept away and pushed into the water, into the gutter.

She went home cold and exhausted; the only feeling that was left inside her head was the movement of the brooms sweeping Paris in the morning.

And as soon as she reached her room she burst out sobbing.

Montmartre Cemetery and Flora and Fauna in Paris

Colette

6 November 1913

This place holds no secrets, yet it is not without its surprises. The throngs of people, the flowers, the children being dragged along—it has a busy, Sunday-ish feel to it, not very reverent. All these people seem to have come along, as I have myself, in a spirit of indifference. I don't 'know' anyone here. The Caulaincourt bridge, which shakes when the trucks and buses cross over it, does nothing for the funeral grandeur of the place. This is just an odd sort of garden, a toy-town consisting of midget houses, chapels like huts, and mausoleums like shacks, all built out of massive stone, iron, or marble, all fashioned and carved in cheerful bad taste and with a childish self-importance which, instead of winning you over, makes you shrug and give a cynical laugh, turning the ritual visit into an indecent sort of outing.

How to describe the enamelled, chocolate-coloured fortresses decorated with mouldings and small round windows, except that they are like the entrance to Magic City? And whatever are we to make of those yellow ceramic rings stuck on the railings or leaning against the blocks of granite? There are some on almost every tomb. The Living throw them to the Dead like rings of toasted golden bread, never again to be crunched by those toothless, lipless mouths. 'Here, have another one! Catch this! You can have another next year!' We can't give them all real flowers, there wouldn't be enough to go round. In this one cemetery alone there are so many, so many Dead. They encroach on the paths, jostle for space, suddenly halt the Living in their tracks by squashing them in between two railed enclosures which almost touch one another. But this is of no concern to the Living, be they man or woman, who squeeze through with some irritation, pulling back their coats, just as they might in a crowded department store . . . .

So many Dead. Yes, under this bridge, next to the road, beside us, among us. Here the Dead are so close, and not much covered by the wood, the lead, the earth. Wood crumbles away, lead goes into holes, the earth sucks in air . . . . I do not quite shiver, but I am chary of this lush soil sticking to my shoes. I am suspicious of the smell in the wind, I loathe the idea of a charnel house being allowed to exist here in the midst of the city, lying in between a new hotel and a picture palace .... When our time comes and we ourselves, obedient, joyous, and ready, have to make that leap, to destroy and purify and scatter our own disgusting remains, let our charnel house be Fire.

But then, what would become of the cult of the Dead, as understood by that good lady over there standing in a proprietorial manner over her small patch and treading all over one, two, three, four slabs engraved with names and dates? She is giving the neck of an urn a thorough going-over with her little brush, scratching the moss away, sweeping it up, pinching out a late shoot from the rose bush, muttering under her breath and clicking her tongue: 'Tut, tut, these servants!' Then she picks up her brush and her gloves again, checks her hat is on straight, examines her reflection in the convex medallion of a string of pearls, and off she goes, with a look of disgust at the luxuriant ivy, thorns, and russet brambles freely establishing their stranglehold on an abandoned green tombstone.

Flora and Fauna of Paris and Elsewhere

'Do you go for a walk every morning?'

'Every morning.'

'What about when the weather's bad?'

'Then I go walking when the weather's bad.'

'Always in the Bois de Boulogne?'

'Always in the Bois de Boulogne.'

At this point my interviewer glances at me quizzically and usually adds: 'Don't you get bored? I should find that deadly.'

He's quite right. The Bois is not so very big. Year by year urban greed finds a way of nibbling at it round the edges, or depleting it in the middle. Whether it be the fortresses of the boulevard Maréchal Manoury, the lamentable boxlike buildings on the Boulevard Suchet, the great ramparts overhanging Bagatelle, the festivals at night or the racecourse by day, it's always the Bois that is forced to give up space or privacy, always the Bois that has to pay the price. And eight days or a month of walking in the Bois doesn't sound much fun, I grant you.

But I've experienced the Bois for something like thirty years, and that makes all the difference. In thirty years the Bois has become my friend, new each day, like a much-loved dwelling, or the moods of the sea, or like when sunlight moves across a wall. A sudden change of mood in the wind, ruffling it, instantly alters the shade of green, my choice of path, the sky, the scent of the earth underfoot and the grass. The acacia season does not flower in the same way as the season of the lime blossom. I could never mistake the perfume of the catalpa for the sickly privet. The great cherry trees with the satin trunks, from which I gather flavoursome little fruits, do not grow in the same areas as the exotic walnuts that in autumn give me the very hard nuts with compact flesh that are well protected by their bitter husk and stain my fingers. As for the mushrooms, I let an expert harvest them. He beats about with his stick in the undergrowth as if he were hunting for vipers. He also digs up the little wild garlic and makes soup out of it, which he praises inordinately. I don't know his name, but I know him by sight. He talks in a wondering sort of way about plants, about what the weather will probably be, and about 'what goes well with bread . . .'. We old wood folk, we don't ask any more of each other than that.

What else do you want to know about the flora? Each spring sees the pillaging of the wild cherry, the elder and blackthorn flowers. I shall certainly not tell you where to find a few spindly but highly scented lilacs unconfined by fences and railings, or the pink corolla of the japonica . . . . In the direction of Auteuil there are still bluebells, as blue as the ones that grow in profusion in April in the woods at Rambouillet and Fausses-Reposes, but they are poor specimens, and in any case Parisians pick them all when they are in bud.

As for the fauna, it is richer than you might imagine. In the season when the starlings return, hundreds of them cover the trees lining the racecourse at Auteuil, and nothing is sweeter than their collective twittering; it is rather like the rustling of silk, a shower of rain, the wind under the door . . . . A few weeks ago, during a bright spell in a false spring, two hundred greenfinches rose up from under my feet, green as jade in the sunshine, like willow and euphorbia. In summer you may spot an incautious hedgehog, the odd slow-worm, a grass snake, some very pretty rats with gold-fawn backs and seagulls, which come up the Seine from the sea. In front of my eyes a warden picked up a little rabbit that was still warm, drained of blood, and more or less decapitated by a stoat . . . . We also have a good number of lost dogs that preoccupied horse riders scatter in their wake, or are forgotten by ladies in a hurry, worried about their hygiene.

Rainy mornings, bluer than when it's fine, rose-coloured mornings like new copper, tarnished by hoarfrost. May mornings, when everything is stirring, unfurling in the vegetation, and there is a feverish activity of beaks and wings, silkworms swaying on the ends of their invisible threads of silk—I only like being in the Bois during the best part of the day, and the only fault I find with the Bois is that it is at times either too deserted or not deserted enough.

What lovely places they would be for relaxation, these great expanses of forest, mixed oak, pine, and acacias, with their paths just wide enough for a foot, if there were not a man, who is neither beggar, mushroom-gatherer, poet, nor criminal standing a hundred metres away. He is not out walking, he is not going anywhere. But he seems to be waiting for all the women who are on their own. As soon as a woman sees him, he sets off in the same direction as she does, and stops if she stops. If she walks at a good pace he loses heart and falls behind. How many times do you see men like this dubious inhabitant of the woods? He does not belong to that category of monomaniacs you could call harmless—as though any monomaniac were harmless. This doubtful character, silent and irresolute, hanging around among the trees, does not block anyone's path. But at the sight of him, the young girl taking a short cut with her racquet tucked under her arm, goes back to the asphalt path, and the woman with the five Pekinese, the lady with the seven fox terriers, the lady with the four chows call in their pack as if there were a fire. What could these walkers complain of? That the man lurking is not committing an offence? The anxiety he instils in them cannot easily be defined. Women are afraid of him, and don't dare say so. All in all they would much prefer to meet the classic 'satyr' pursued by the wardens, the one who causes such indignation in the last of that dying breed of eagle-eyed mothers.

Last year, on the path round the lower lake, one mother chaperoning her daughter, garrulous and panting for breath, was appealing to a warden in bottle green: 'Look, if the Bois de Boulogne in the middle of the day is not somewhere where families can go walking, if a young girl, even when she's with her mother, runs the risk of meeting the worst kind of . . . of . . . person . . . .'

The green warden, who in any case would have been unable to get a word in, said nothing. But her calm, willowy daughter was sagely pulling at her mother's sleeve: 'Leave it, Mother, come on, we shall be late. In any case, you know I'm short-sighted.'

The Gare Saint-Lazare

Michel Butor

After photographs by Jean-Philippe Charbonnier

1

So we managed to catch it once more; touch and go; the train was already in as we were going down the steps, as we were going up the steps; the carriage was full already, as it was every morning, and you had to force all those other people arriving, flowing along in a slowly moving river to move up even more; you had to use your shoulders to persuade them, so that you could squeeze in, your coats brushing against each other, and allow the doors to close before the jolting began again,

full, as it was every day, but surely it was colder than yester-day, perhaps the heating had gone wrong again, as it did almost every day, so while we were stationary, and the number of people steadily increased and more and more kept nudging their way in, forcing us to squash up still more so that we could all fit in, a damp gust of cold morning air swept through our hair momentarily, steam came out of our mouths, we rubbed our hands together and cracked our joints because, for the first time in many days, we had left our gloves behind,

2

—I should have got the earlier train, that one really is cutting it a bit fine, they're bound to say something. It all depends whether we get held up or not. It depends on . . . As though there weren't hold-ups every day! Can you remember a day when there weren't any hold-ups? Sunday, ah yes, of course, but that was Sunday. He'll say: So, can't you do anything about it? Can't you get here on time like everyone else? I do realize how delightful your little house and garden are . . . But, as I've already told you dozens of times, there aren't many firms who would allow you to . . .

for out in the suburbs in the early morning, it had looked as if it was going to be rather fine, a touch of spring in the air, and some of the more optimistic among us had not even brought coats with them, assuming it would be sunny this afternoon, and although it's true that it's definitely not so cold now and you are all right in just a jacket, as far as blue sky is concerned, which we shouldn't be able to see in any case through these dirty station windows, those of us about to spill out on to the square after handing the ticket-collector our tickets or the cards we are clutching or hunting for anxiously in one pocket or another, as we do every morning

3

—Stay by me, darling. As long as I've got my arm round you, you needn't worry, all you have to do is keep your eyes open and watch where you're going, keep your eyes on the people, the cars, and the roofs; the thing is, here, it's not like at home; everything is a completely different size and if you were to wander off, and I lost you, where would you go in all this crowd of people, in this mad rush, in the noise? Stay by me and we'll be all right, you'll see, we'll be able to cross, you'll see, and go to that big store, brightly lit and swarming with people, and buy you that new pair of shoes, the sort you can't get at home, and buy that new blouse for me and the seeds for the garden. The traffic policeman will get everyone moving in the right direction. They are fighting, but it's only words; he's still young, you understand, and rather inexperienced. Then we'll go and have something to eat in the department store; there is a big restaurant with stools like in America, and you can have an ice-cream for dessert while I have a coffee

(one ought to just get into the habit, too silly of me to be worried about it every day like this; from today I shall put it, or them, in my purse, that's the most obvious place, but now I come to think, I haven't looked in my purse, perhaps that's where it is, or they are, and yesterday I remember in fact telling myself that from today...

—Tomorrow we'll take the earlier train, because if we have to be in such a rush all the time... We are bound to ladder our stockings.
—I told you we should have got the earlier train, but I had to wait half an hour; you were taking such an age to do your hair...

the blue sky, those who are going to come out on to the Rue d'Amsterdam or on to the square, coming down the stairs beyond the hall, or some just beyond the concourse, won't find a trace of it, so here it is, another grey, cloudy day, and no doubt rainy, just to cap it all, the minute we get outside

—Stay beside me, darling. Don't worry, the traffic jam will sort itself out. Come a bit closer still. As you can see, the briefcase I'm holding is the one I gave you; I use it every day. If I could speak, if there were really any point in speaking in all this tumult of people leaving work and getting swallowed up by buses and métros on empty stomachs, I would say how much I love that slender strand of hair, which meets the arch of your eyebrows before inclining downwards towards your ear, and if we still have to wait a few more moments before we move, and even arrive a few minutes late at your dreadful parents' place in the Rue

Tronchet, I should bless that nice inexperienced policeman for having given us this one minute's fragile peace and quiet in the middle of all this crowd. I can see him out of the corner of my eye, showing off, wanting to be admired . . .

(all the same it's quite ridiculous of me not to have picked up my raincoat before I left; everyone here, well at least nearly everyone, has had the sense to bring their raincoats; I must ask my husband if he'll buy me another one with a floral design like that one, if one could be found, that is, where the flowers were not quite so pink—I must ask my wife to come with me and buy another raincoat because actually the one I left at home . . . and I am incapable of buying one on my own,

—I'd love to know where you got your raincoat; I suppose a white raincoat like that . . .
—Well funnily enough, I wanted a black raincoat. We should swap for the afternoon.
—But you know quite well I'm a lot taller than you.
—Or what about a white raincoat like that one?
—Where?
—Behind you, that woman waiting.
—With the black gloves and the bracelet?
—Quick, come on, the signal's green.

Or else a leather jacket, that's definitely warm and practical, only it's a different sort of thing, I couldn't wear a leather jacket to the office—that girl with a leather jacket—a raincoat or an umbrella) those of us, for, in the main, the escalators will take us much farther down beyond the Rue d'Amsterdam or the level below the square, and we shall have to wait again behind the automatic gates and on platforms, and start pushing our way into other carriages once more,

> —He's good-looking; what a pity he's a policeman. The peaked cap suits him so well, but it would be better if it belonged to a cavalry officer. There I go, seduced by men in uniform again . . . . I think it's time to go home. And he's really young, and rather sensitive I should say; he must make lots of conquests. He's not looking at the taxi driver any more, but at that woman wanting to cross; he's trying to dominate, to seduce her. Or am I being silly?

And it's already time to search handbags, wallets and dig deep into pockets for more tickets and more cards.

> —in the crowd of shoes one white toe, one black; for a fraction of a second it's as if these two legs belonged to the same extraordinarily bold and elegant person, describing an exquisite dance movement for one single spectator hidden among the multitude of people who are paying no attention.
> —She fiddles impatiently with her handbag; she rises slowly on tiptoe, stretching her foot right out, flexing

all her muscles, and then staying up as long as possible, to make the moment last.

—I'm here, darling, you don't have to say anything; if my hair is a mess, it's just because I've been running so fast; I thought the class would never end. When I left the house this morning I put two new ribbons nice and flat between two sheets in my folder and I was going to tie them on the end of my plaits . . .

—He's not there. Although he said he would be in Paris this morning, and he always uses that exit when he arrives. The next train is in a quarter of an hour; he must have missed this one; or else he may have got the one before, but that would be odd. Unless he did it deliberately because . . . or he went out by another exit because . . . or else he told me deliberately he was coming to Paris, but . . .

—Not exactly the right time to start flirting, is it! That's all they do these young policemen, but as to directing the traffic . . . It's true things are getting worse and worse, but all the same in my young days when I used to come to Paris, the policemen I saw as I came out of the Gare Saint-Lazare were different altogether; they didn't need to start flirting with people in the middle of the street . . .

4

—Well obviously, with shoes like that!
—And in this weather!

—How stupid we've been!

—Well yes, darling, I'm afraid we've ruined them . . .

—Especially yours, they are starting to come apart . . .

—Don't start, right?

—It's a disaster, and that's that . . .

—They'll just about do for the beach . . . .

> —She's not there. If she thinks she's going to be able to carry on standing me up like that! This is at least the third or fourth time, and always excuses, pretexts, and then like an idiot, I give in . . . But she ought to realize she needs me a lot more than I need her. I may have put on a bit of weight recently, but I am perfectly capable, yes, perfectly capable of managing on my own; all the same she ought to know that in Paris, and especially in this area, there's no shortage of girls around, girls of all kinds, who would certainly not mind finding somebody to look after them a bit and be nice to them, and who wouldn't haggle about certain things, and even if at a pinch I was obliged to help them out a bit financially, I wonder if in the end it wouldn't work out cheaper for me . . .

—Look, we'll get over it . . .

—It was that ray of sunshine this morning, I thought it was going to turn out fine . . .

—There's only one thing to be done now, go back home . . .

—I wonder what she can be taking photos of; she must be American . . .

—Well, believe it or not, what he said to me when I got back . . .

> —Do you like ice-cream?
> —Aren't you getting a bit hungry?
> —I'm watching the water run along the gutter.
> —Are we a long way from home, do you know?
> —Mum's waiting for a taxi.
> —Take care of your white gloves, be careful of your white shoes.
> —I think the jacket she's got over her arm is shammy leather.
> —Are these commuters, all these people getting off?
> —No, they're from outside Paris.

—She talks and talks, she can't stop talking. But I am sucking, kissing the handle of my umbrella very gently, and beginning to think . . .

—It's getting late, I wonder what it'll be like, the light is going . . .

—It's starting to rain, so for goodness' sake walk along without moaning!

—The first big drops, but I'm absolutely sure it's going to pour . . .

—Except that with my shoes in this state I wonder how on earth I'm going to get there . . .

> That flowered print, for example, that white belt, three-quarter sleeves, wristwatch, the way her hands

hang down, her sweater, no, not a sweater but a white, knitted jacket that buttons up, carefully balanced on her handbag, her way of walking so slowly, the way she moves her hips, her feet dragging along the ground, and she's certainly not lacking in self-assurance, she looks as if she were going to stop, as if she has noticed me; yes, she has, it's definitely me she's looking at and all I should have to do . . .

—Is he going to speak to her or isn't he? I wonder if he'll make up his mind. Behind his back his other hand is squeezing his index finger; she is not saying a word, dancing around first on one foot, then the other, swaying back and forth like a slender tree or the sail on a ship. She turns, now to the left, now a little to the right, breathes in deeply, seeing how the land lies and returns to her indolent walking to and fro, and the fat little man's right hand has escaped in her direction but she is no longer looking at him . . .

—And here's the Gare Saint-Lazare. It's six-eleven, I've plenty of time, especially since I've got my return ticket . . .

—My scar always starts itching in weather like this . . .

—Another day over . . .

—I'll be home for supper . . .

—It'll be raining all the way, but she will have made some coffee, and lit the fire . . .

—The advert says: All-leather shoes, but my feet are already soaked . . .

—Supposing we go to a film tonight, that might do us good, don't you think ... ?

5

... because if we want to have a bite to eat in the station concourse, considering everything that's slowing us down, our rheumatism, our sneezes, our coughs, all this weight of the day we are dragging around, all the dust we have swallowed, all this noise we have had to put up with—and it's not over yet—all this crowd we have been carried along by

(oh, if only now we might be carried along a little faster, if we could climb these high, steep, hard, pitiless steps with a little less effort!)

—Supper in the buffet or restaurant ...

—Go back to my room and work or ...

—Don't forget to buy a few flowers, or ...

—Every time I come back from this cemetery, it's the same old thing; and there's no point me bringing back his big framed photograph ...

—Where's the twenty-seven bus go to then? I don't think I've ever caught it ...

—Here's the ninety-five at last!

and even quite simply without having the time to sit down, to grab a sandwich—ham? Gruyère? sausage?—to munch it ravenously while you queue outside the ticket office, for there are a lot of us without return tickets

(—What on earth can they have to say to each other?

—It's easy enough to buy a ticket, for heaven's sake!

—He's taking his time sorting out his change!

—This purse, I can't open it with all this in my hands!

—Put the windscreen-wipers on, I can't see a thing.

—Get a move on! Your homework has to be done.

—How awful he's been all day, and fancy me having brought him up!

—It's a drop of water fallen into my eye.

—It's a bit of grit.

—You couldn't see a thing just now; they really could have put the lights on earlier!

—This is what we call 'the time between dog and wolf'.[1]

—Slip this little piece of cardboard in between your lips . . .); and yes, you're right, we perhaps should have accepted that invitation

(but later it's so dark and lonely on our streets and on the main roads),

or take time between two bits of shopping, in the tea-room or snack-bar . . .

---

[1] A literal translation of the French expression.

(but we wanted to make the most of it, to look, compare, feel, choose, find out about it until closing time),
and it'll be such a long way on an empty stomach, in the rain . . .

> —You see, the good thing about Paris, and I should know because I've seen heaps of foreign cities, is that you can have a snack like this sitting outside while you watch the world go by.
> —He's finally managed to drag himself away, the two little girls and their mother, the two lovers, the two eaters of ice-cream, will finally be able to get across.
> —These sandwiches are a bit stale; you need wine to help them down . . .

and there are plenty of us who, when we do get to the top of the steps in the concourse, will be twice as tired, but not very surprised, to see that in spite of all our efforts, and sweat, and being out of breath, it's too late to catch the train we had decided upon (it was because of the taxi, the métro, our friend . . .) that we would need another twenty minutes or half an hour, phone home to tell them not to wait, to start the meal, that it doesn't matter . . .

> —You see, when they have a sale on here, you've got to arrive in good time; in the afternoon there's nothing left . . .

and some of us are not rushing to the ticket office, the buffet, or the train, but towards a meeting point, looking all round, hearts beating with each shape that reminds us a little . . . hearts sinking a little more with every minute that goes by after the time we had arranged

>—All the signs on the square . . .
>—And the streetlamps all at once . . .
>—The car lights pair by pair . . .
>—And the station windows . . .
>—Reflected in the wet pavement . . .
>—In the streaming bodywork and the shop windows . . .
>—It must be a woman driver . . .
>—Those brakes . . .
>—That skid . . .
>—The policeman's whistle . . .
>—Our turn to cross.

(perhaps he'll stay in Paris tonight; he told me not to absolutely count on him, that if he wasn't there on time it was because . . . but if I get the train now and he arrives in just a moment and doesn't find me, he will perhaps be . . . he'll say . . . no, he won't say anything, he will only say that I was right to go home without him, but he will think . . . and if he doesn't think, if I'm making it all up . . . oh, I wish so much he would come now, and if I get the train on my own when he's perhaps on the escalator and wants nothing more than to . . . Oh, I'll catch the next train).

—Darling, the rain will wash away our bad feelings, don't you think . . . ?

(—So there you are? You're absolutely soaked!

—So what have you been doing today?

—You told me you would get the one before; I'd given up expecting you. They're not waiting for you, are they?

—My parents? I phoned them. I was late too.

—And what time did you say you'd arrive?

—By the next one, obviously; but it doesn't greatly matter, they'll have started without me . . .

—So then, what would you rather do, have supper here or there?)

He's been trying to pay for quarter of an hour; you are surely not going to make him miss his train!

and the very last, those of us who have accepted invitations, been to the theatre, concert, cinema, those who have dragged themselves away from their friends, saying, 'I've got to catch my train' and those to whom we have shown sympathy, saying 'you have a garden, fresh air, peace and quiet', they are the ones who have to make most haste in the gloomy station now emptying, haunted by the ghost of a crowd, for this time it really is the last departure and on no account must they miss it . . .

The Twentieth Arrondissement

Léon-Paul Fargue

The twentieth *arrondissement*, where our game of Paris Mother Goose ends,[1] is in a way—because of Père-Lachaise—also where it reaches its spiritual conclusion. Paris, in this quasi-poetic, quasi-administrative domain, with its memories and its ghosts, begins at the Louvre and finishes at Ménilmontant. There is no water in the twentieth, nor any rail network, and the only thing that might put you in mind of water, or the infinite, is the notorious Rue des Pyrénées which cuts right through it from top to bottom. This is the equivalent of the Rue de Vaugirard or the Rue Saint-Honoré, as full of numbers as a telephone directory. There the oddest kinds of houses, right down to the

---

[1] This is the last of Fargue's evocations of the twenty Paris *arrondissements*.

simplest cottage with its tiny onion patch, jostle bravely for their place in the sun of the capital. To the northeast of Couronnes métro station, squashed in between the blocks of houses, you can still see a kind of no-man's-land where people do not have electricity. There they use paraffin for their lighting, when they can get any, otherwise candles. Outside the low, windowless houses, there are little fences like the ones you see in villages, or like the ones clowns sometimes use to make their entrance into the ring more convoluted. This quiet backwater was for a long time the refuge of the Communards,[2] the last heroes, the last families of the Commune; and in the old days, when it was my habit to walk the whole of Paris, I used to surprise and delight many of my friends when I took them up there. Afterwards we would go down towards Ménilmontant, towards the Flemish church in the Avenue Philippe-Auguste, sometimes in the direction of Gambetta and Bagnolet, and the Tenon Hospital where there held sway—in the old days—the most colourful guild of medical students in the university life of Paris. The twentieth *arrondissement* is the country of Bruant,[3] more than the nineteenth is. His most powerful, most 'sincere' songs, as they say, expose in an emphatic fashion the modes and

---

[2] The citizens who rose up against the government from March to May 1871 after France's defeat in the Franco-Prussian War and the collapse of Napoleon III's Second Empire, 1852–70.

[3] Aristide Bruant, a friend of Toulouse-Lautrec, was famous for the songs in which he espoused the cause of the social underclass. He owned a cabaret called '*Le Mirliton*'. '*Pante*' is an archaic word meaning 'rustic' or 'peasant'.

manners of Charonne, Tourelles, and Ménilmontant. His notorious *pantes* were from around here.

The tourist may be disappointed in this area, and we need not be ashamed to say so, for sites of interest are few and far between: neither the Place Saint-Fargeau, tucked in beside the reservoirs of Ménilmontant, the church of Notre Dame de la Croix, the Square Séverine, the Square Sarah-Bernhardt, the Debrousse Hospice, nor the Place de la Réunion will tempt the art lover. But those who find what is gentle and picturesque appealing will discover a multitude of things to savour, and, now and again, facets that will delight you by their very ordinariness. A film-maker could make the most instructive of forays into this area. Here there is a street corner pulsating with life, a Saint-Honoré full of rooftops and studios, and shadowy dwellings from which the notes of an accordion, like a great flapping of birds, fly off into the air. Flowers, that look like the little heads of schoolchildren playing truant, peep out from the struts beneath the windows. You become accustomed to the sight of garages, laundries, small factories. The brash noises and the variety theatre are quite in keeping in this fresco where I, at any rate, have made so many instant friends, met so many brother poets, albeit just by having watched them at work, or deep in thought. We may not speak the same language, but we have suffered in the same manner. And no doubt we have had exactly the same feelings when we heard sailors singing in the hooting of the buses or the whine of the sirens.

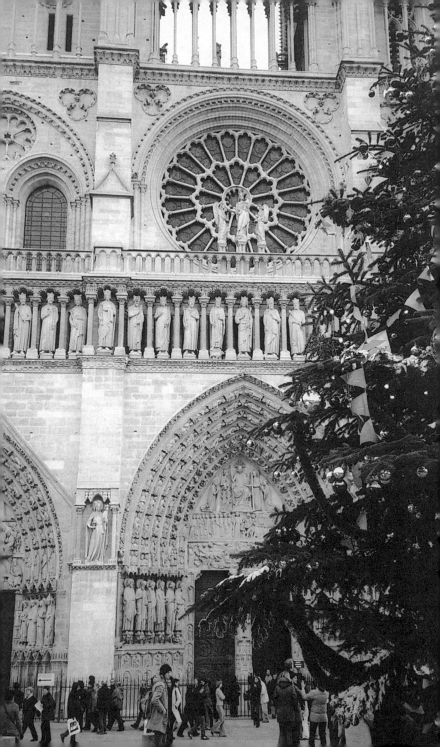

In Notre-Dame

Julien Green

Every now and then inanimate objects seem suddenly empowered to speak to us, to cry out to us in a language that is more or less incomprehensible, and communicate messages whose meaning only becomes clear when it is too late. It is as if matter receives the gift of seeing into the future and prophesies, whenever it is so inclined; to no effect, for who ever heeds the words of a prophet?

One Thursday of Holy Week in 1940,[1] as night was drawing in, I found myself in Notre-Dame. Some of the cathedral treasures, the relics, were on display: the nails, if I remember rightly, and, I think, a piece of the crown of

---

[1] That is, during the Occupation of Paris in the Second World War.

thorns. Four or five people, at most, were meditating in front of these objects. Above their heads an electric bulb threw out harsh rays of light into the blackness enveloping the nave. To the right and left of the little makeshift altar, I could see men draped in white cloaks; but, although they looked most odd, they were not the first thing to attract my attention, for what astonished me much more was what I could hear. Now around the relics a sort of zone of silence, whose boundaries you could have mapped out, transformed those five square yards into a place of ineffable solitude. High up in the transept, however, a mighty tumult raged. The panes in the great rose-window on the north side had been removed, and in their place was a large piece of sheeting into which the wind plunged with a kind of muffled blast resembling cannon fire. They were the last gales of the winter and they were shaking the huge grey canvas as if to break it into little pieces. In the howling of the storm I thought I could hear only the accents of rage and despair but, as I was listening to this mournful, splendid sound, I noticed that the deep peace encircling the small band of worshippers was not in the least disturbed by it. It was like when you see trees sometimes bow their heads beneath a gust of wind, while three or four yards below them the flowers and leaves of the bushes remain perfectly still. The tremendous voice striking against the arches and filling the nave with the noise of battle broke against an invisible wall some feet from the ground, and you could have heard, or so it seemed, at one and the same time, the whisper of a page being turned and that great clamour, which was like a combination of shouting crowds and hundreds of tanks rumbling past.

It was then that I turned my attention to the men in white. They were sitting opposite one another, wrapped in those enormous capes whose colour reminded me of the beautiful churches in Touraine. Each wore a big black cross embroidered on his right shoulder, and I thought I could detect the effort of meditation in their faces, which were marked by great solemnity. I was thinking vaguely of the knights of the Holy Sepulchre,[2] when suddenly it came to me that these men and women had gathered for a ceremony whose meaning escaped them and that in actual fact they were watching for somebody. It was as if the wind, the twilight, the pillars and arches, the whole cathedral were crying out a terrible warning that we could not hear. I went out almost immediately, not suspecting that I should not see Notre-Dame again for another five years . . .

The other day I went back. It was November. It was icy cold on my back and I went forward into the half-light as if into the middle of a wood. There is no part of Paris that is not haunted by my memories. Here I remembered the kind

---

[2] An order of knights so called because they were dubbed at the tomb of the Holy Sepulchre in Jerusalem.

of awe that possessed my whole being when, holding my mother's hand, I used to enter the ancient church. Every child is a little savage, and like the savage that I was, I found so much grandeur overwhelming. And still today, however much I love Notre-Dame, I feel intimidated by her profundity, her echoes, and by all the darkness she contains within her.

As soon as I was in the transept, I lifted up my eyes to the rose-window on the north side and ascertained that the big grey sheet was still hanging there, but there was no wind to blow it around, and instead of the voice of the storm I could hear the much more reassuring murmur of the canons intoning the service. Then I recalled the knights of the Holy Sepulchre and the women on their knees in front of the relics. How distant it all seemed to me now, and how bizarre the fearful question I had asked myself that day: 'So who are they watching for?'

As I glanced around the cathedral, I was brought up short. Something clutched at my throat. What I saw, I was not expecting, but recognized straight away. In the south transept, high, naked, and in all its overpowering simplicity, rose the wooden cross commemorating the dead of Buchenwald.[3] There it was, waiting and watching, as objects can wait and watch. For a long time I remained near it,

---

[3] One of the first Nazi concentration camps, near Weimar, Germany.

walking away from it only to retrace my steps and then return once more to take another look. It was like a great howl of pain and indignation. I am sure the Middle Ages would not have found anything else but this to express what words can never say, and I could not help believing that an answer to my troubled question of March 1940 was being granted to me now, in November 1945.

Family Portrait

Maryse Condé

If my parents had been asked what they thought of the Second World War they would have promptly replied that they were the darkest times they had ever known. Not because of France being divided into two, the camps at Drancy or Auschwitz, or the extermination of six million Jews, nor because of all the crimes against humanity that we have not yet finished paying for, but because for seven long years they were deprived of what was the most important thing in their lives: their trips to France. As my father was a former state employee and my mother was in practice, they regularly enjoyed holidays in the 'metropolis' with their children.

In their eyes France was in no sense that seat of colonial power. It was the true motherland and Paris was the City of

Light and the light of their lives. My mother stuffed our heads full of descriptions of the wonders of the market at Temple and Saint-Pierre and first and foremost the Sainte-Chapelle and Versailles. My father preferred the Louvre museum and the Cigale dance hall where he went to shake a leg when he was a boy. So, when we were halfway through the year 1946, they took great delight in boarding the steamer that would convey them to the port of Le Havre, the first port of call on the return journey to their adoptive country.

I was the baby of the family. One of our family myths concerned my arrival into the world. My father was an upright man of sixty-three. My mother had just celebrated her forty-first birthday. When her bleeding stopped she thought it was the first signs of the menopause and hurried off to see her gynaecologist, Doctor Melas, who had delivered her seven children. When he examined her he laughed out loud.

'I felt so ashamed,' my mother told her friends, 'that during the early months of pregnancy I felt like an unmarried mother. I tried to hide my belly in front of me.'

It was no good her adding, as she kissed me effusively, that her *kras a boyo*[1] had become her support in her old age. I still felt the same old pang each time I heard it. I had not been wanted.

---

[1] A derogatory term in Creole used to describe a child born to older parents.

Today I can still see what an odd spectacle we must have presented, sitting outside the cafés in the Latin Quarter in the dreary Paris of the post-war years. My father, who had once been very handsome and attractive; my mother covered in sumptuous creole jewels; us eight children, my sisters with downcast eyes, dressed up to the nines, my teenage brothers, one of whom was already in his first year of medicine, and myself, an impossibly spoilt and precocious child. The waiters, balancing their trays on their hips, buzzed around us like honey bees, filled with admiration. They served us mint diabolos, remarking, 'What excellent French you speak!'

My parents accepted this compliment without flinching or smiling and contented themselves with a nod. Once the waiters' backs were turned they called us to witness: 'And we're as French as they are,' my father sighed.

'More French,' my mother added vehemently. And by way of explanation she continued: 'We are more educated. We have better manners. We have read more. Some of them have never set foot outside Paris, whereas we have been to the Mont Saint-Michel, the Côte d'Azur, and the Côte Basque.'

In this exchange there was a certain pathos, which always cut me to the quick even though I was so young. They were complaining of a grave injustice. Roles were reversed, illogically. The waiters in their black waistcoats and white aprons scooping up their tips considered themselves superior to their generous customers. By their very nature they possessed a French identity that was denied to my parents, despite their respectable appearance. And as for me, I did not understand what it was that caused my proud parents, who were so happy, and held such important positions in their own country, to try to compete with those who were waiting on them.

One day I decided to sort the matter out. I turned to my brother Alexander—Sandrino as he had re-christened himself 'to sound more American'—as I did every time I was troubled about something. Top of his class, pockets stuffed full of love-letters from his little girlfriends, Sandrino was the sun in my sky. Like the good brother he was, he behaved with an affectionate protectiveness towards me. But I wasn't content with just being his little sister, forgotten as soon as some girl with a figure like an hourglass walked past, or whenever a football match started. Did he understand why our parents behaved like that? Why did they so much envy people who, as they said themselves, were quite below them?

We stayed in a ground-floor flat in a quiet street in the seventh *arrondissement*. It wasn't like being in La Pointe,[2] where we were firmly locked up and imprisoned in our

---

[2] Pointe-à-Pitre, the capital town of Guadeloupe.

house. Here our parents allowed us to go out as much as we liked and even to play with other children. At that time I was astonished at such freedom. Later I realized that in France our parents were not afraid we would start talking Creole or take up banging *gwokas*[3] like the little black children in La Pointe. As I remember, that day we had been playing hide-and-seek with the blond children from upstairs and sharing a tea that consisted of dried fruit, for Paris was still in straitened circumstances. Night was beginning to transform the sky into a starry sieve. We were getting ready to go home before one of my sisters could poke her head out of the window and shout: 'Children! Mum and Dad say you've got to come in.'

Sandrino leaned in the doorway. His jovial face, still childishly chubby, assumed a dark expression. His voice became more serious. He answered: 'Don't bother your head about it,' he said. 'Mum and Dad are a couple of aliens.'[4]

Aliens? What did that mean? I dared not ask. It wasn't the first time I'd heard Sandrino make jokes at my parents' expense. My mother had hung a photo she had cut out of *Ebony* above her bed. There for all to admire was a black American family of eight children, like ours. All of them were doctors, lawyers, engineers, architects. In short, the

---

[3] A Creole drum

[4] '*Aliéné*' in French also has connotations of being psychologically unbalanced.

pride and joy of their parents. Sandrino relentlessly made fun of this photo, for, unaware of the fact that he would die before he had even begun to live his life, he swore he would become a famous writer. He hid from me the first pages of his novel, but often recited his poems, which left me struggling, since, according to him, poetry was incomprehensible.

I spent the following night tossing and turning in my bed, at the risk of waking my sister Thérèse who was sleeping above my head. For one thing I adored my mother and father. I wasn't keen on their greying hair, of course, or the wrinkles on their foreheads. I should have preferred them both to be young. If only they would take my mother for my big sister, like they did with my best friend Yvelise when her mum went to catechism with her. And it was excruciating for me to hear my father adorning his conversation with Latin phrases, which I later discovered could be found in the *Petit Larousse illustré*. *Verba volent. Scripta manent. Carpe diem. Pater familias. Deus ex machina.*[5] And worst of all were the stockings, two shades too light for her dark skin, that Mother wore when the weather was hot. But I knew how much they loved us, and that they were making an effort to prepare us for what they believed to be the best of all possible lives.

---

[5] *Speech flies away. Written words remain. Seize the moment. Father of the family. The god out of the machine.*

At the same time my trust in my brother was too implicit to cast doubts on his judgement. From his expression and tone of voice, I sensed that the mysterious word 'alien' denoted a kind of shameful infection, like gonorrhoea, even perhaps a fatal one like typhoid fever, which had claimed the lives of so many people at La Pointe the previous year. At midnight, by dint of piecing together all the clues, I ended up constructing a sort of theory. An alien is someone who tries to be what he cannot be because he doesn't like what he is. At two o'clock in the morning, just as I was drifting off to sleep, I made a rather muddled vow to myself that I would never become an alien.

As a result, when I woke up I was a changed girl. From having been a model child I became argumentative and started answering back. As I wasn't sure what my aims and ambitions were, I simply questioned everything my parents suggested. An evening at the Opéra to listen to the trumpets of *Aida* or the bells of *Lakmé*. A visit to the Orangerie to admire Monet's water lilies. Or just a dress, a pair of shoes, or ribbons for my hair. My mother, who was not renowned for her patience, didn't stint on the slaps. Twenty times a day she would exclaim: 'Now what on earth has got into that girl?'

A photo taken at the end of that stay in France shows us in the Luxembourg gardens. My brothers and sisters all lined up in a row. My father, with a moustache, wearing a coat with a fur collar. My smiling mother, showing all her pearly white teeth, her almond eyes stretched beneath her grey taupe. And me sitting between her legs, skinny, rendered ugly by the sulky, fed-up expression that I was to cultivate until the end of my adolescence, when fate, whose blows are always too hard on ungrateful children, made an orphan of me at the age of twenty.

Since then, I have had all the time in the world to understand the meaning of the word alien, and especially to wonder if Sandrino was right. Were my parents aliens? It is an absolute certainty that they were not proud of their African heritage. They were wholly ignorant of it, and that's a fact! During those times in France my father never went down to the Rue des Écoles, the home of the magazine *Présence africaine*, the brainchild of Alioune Diop.[6] Like my mother, he was convinced that it was only Western culture that was worth having and was grateful to France for allowing them access to it. At the same time neither one nor the other experienced the slightest sense of inferiority because of their colour. They thought of themselves as being most brilliant and intelligent, the overwhelming proof of the progress of their *Race des Grands-Nègres*.[7]

Is that what it means to be an 'alien'?

---

[6] Alioune Diop, 1910–80, was a key figure in the advancement of black writing in the 1950s. The editorial committee of *Présence africaine* included Jean-Paul Sartre, Albert Camus, and André Gide.

[7] In Guadeloupe the '*petits-nègres*' are the poor, lower class, and the '*grands-nègres*' the rich upper class.

The Runaway

Georges Perec

The stamp market in the Champs-Élysées gardens was only open on Thursdays and Sundays. He knew that, but he said to himself he might meet somebody, some old man with nothing much to do, who would have a look at his album, pausing over the dark brown Blériot or the Victory of Samothrace; someone who would appreciate the set of Mariannes or the scarlet Pétain surcharged with the cross of Lorraine. But there wasn't a single person, nobody walking even. Only metal chairs painted green, in rows between the trees.

It was not yet nine o'clock. The morning was mild. A municipal water-cart was moving along the Avenue Gabriel. The Champs-Élysées looked deserted. On the other side of the gardens, in between the small swings and the puppet theatre, workmen were unloading a roundabout, the frame already assembled.

He sat down on a bench and undid his satchel. He took out the little wallet he used for keeping his swaps in. Long ago he had slipped his best stamps into the little pocket sewn into the binding, from his proper collection in the leather-bound album that his aunt kept under lock and key in the cupboard in her room next to her jewellery, and did not much like him looking at.

He examined them closely, one by one, put them in order, tried to work out how much he would get for them. Later he shut the wallet and placed it in the inside pocket of his jacket.

He took out his timetable. That day, Wednesday, he had an hour of French and an hour of Latin with Monsieur Bourguignon, an hour of history with Monsieur Poirier, an hour of English with Monsieur Normand. In the afternoon an hour's art with Monsieur Joly, an hour of biology with Monsieur Léonard. He hadn't done his English homework, nor prepared his written questions.

It was nine o'clock. He was late, that was all. Everything could still be put right.

He'd missed his first hour many times already. At eight-thirty the caretaker closed the pupils' entrance. He was never brave enough to go through the main entrance in the Avenue du Parc des Princes.

He always came back at nine-thirty. His absence, recorded in the class register, meant two hours' detention on Thursday morning. But the fact that he was late was an alibi: a sin that was a thousand times easier to cope with when confronted by his uncle than the sin of disobedience.

Heady with freedom, he set off for the Porte de Saint-Cloud, Avenue de Versailles. He went into Prisunic, dawdling at all the stands, in front of the hammers, the bowls, the soaps. Sometimes he was fortunate enough to be able to steal a nail, screw, hobnail, or light switch. He opened his books and flicked through them. He read through his exercise books and his old pieces of homework. He opened the green leather pencil-case passed on by his two cousins. It contained a chewed old ruler, three broken coloured pencils, one black pencil, one broken pen stuck together with Elastoplast, a protractor made of Plexiglass, a used eraser, a pair of compasses. He traced out a few circles on the yellow wooden bench. Then he put the compasses back in the pencil-case, and the pencil-case, books, and exercise books into the satchel.

Later he went over to the bushes surrounding the puppet theatre, and when he was sure no one was watching, he pushed aside the branches and dropped his satchel into them. Then he ran away as fast as he could.

He was sitting on a bench opposite the *Figaro* building. The lights in the windows where the newspaper was displayed had finally been put out. The huge capital F, with the goose quill across it, was the only thing left illuminated above the entrance. The park was deserted. You couldn't even make out the blue and orange canopy of the merry-go-round. A few walkers on the Champs-Élysées passed only a couple of yards away, not seeing him, making their way swiftly home. He could hear their voices, faintly. He got up. He crossed the Champs-Élysées, went as far as the métro station. Saw that it was closed and went back again.

He was chilly. He lay down on the bench, curled up as best he could, hugging his bare knees with his arms. The bench, made of two pieces of wood screwed on to cast-iron legs, was too narrow. He got up, walked around, came back and sat down, lay down again, resting his head on his right arm, pressing his knees up against his chest.

He closed his eyes, then opened them again.

A few yards away people passed by like ghosts.

One or two cars drove past behind him, slowed down, changed gear, occasionally hooted.

Later on, a man came towards him. He saw him coming from a long way off, a dark shape against the darker back-cloth of the *Figaro* building. He shut his eyes, pretending to be asleep. His heart was thumping fit to burst.

What are you doing there? the man asked.

He did not answer.

What are you doing there? he asked again. Where do you live?

He did not answer. He looked at him.

The man was tall, well dressed, and he seemed concerned.

For one minute he thought he could tell him, explain what the matter was. But he had nothing to say. He realized he had been waiting all day for this: for someone to speak to him, see him, come and fetch him back.

Leave me alone, he said.

Come on now, come with me, said the man.

He took him by the hand and led him to the police station in the Grand Palais.

I found him on a bench at the roundabout next to the *Figaro*, he told the policemen.

He had twenty-three francs on him. He spent them very quickly. Around the middle of the morning, he went into a bakery in the Rue du Colisée and bought a soft roll for ten francs. He ate it slowly, taking small mouthfuls as he walked along.

A little while later he bought a comic from a kiosk on the Avenue des Champs-Élysées. He went and sat down to read it, but did not enjoy it at all. He had three francs left: one of forty sous, one of twenty, both of them Vichy coins. He would not be able to buy anything with them, except possibly a sweet or a packet of chewing-gum, at a kiosk, but he did not come across one.

Later he found a crumpled copy of *France-Soir* in one of the wastepaper bins in the Alma-Marceau métro station. He looked for the sports page, read the comic strips, the gossip columns, then, tiring of it, threw it down again where he had found it.

Later, much later, he mingled with the people who linger for hours reading the *Figaro*, the *Figaro Littéraire*, and the *Figaro Agricole*, which are posted up on the walls of the offices in the Champs-Élysées.

Later he drank water from a drinking fountain.

His aunt, in her dressing-gown, her hair untidy and her cigarette—first of the day—in her mouth, closed the door after him, a thick, heavy door, with three brass locks and a padlock, that never banged. He began to go downstairs as usual, then stopped, remained there without moving for a few moments between the two landings. He looked at the marble steps, the red carpet, the wrought-iron and the mirrors in the lift cage. He continued his slow descent, letting himself fall almost, from one step to the next, his knees stiff, like a robot or a monster. Head lowered, he went past the caretaker, who, a pipe in his mouth and blue apron round his waist, was polishing up the knobs on the lift with a bit of woollen cloth.

The mirrors in the big hall momentarily sent back reflections of himself into infinity. He went out. The Rue de l'Assomption was tranquil, almost like a street in the provinces, still asleep. The dustbins were unemptied; caretakers were beating the doormats.

The schoolchildren, girls and boys, who went to Janson-de-Sailly or Claude Bernard, to La Fontaine or Molière, were going up the road to the métro Ranelagh, or going down to wait for the number 52 in the Rue de Boulainvilliers.

He took the métro, just as he did every day. He held out his weekly ticket to the ticket-collector; it had already been punched four times and now the conductor punched Wednesday's ticket for the outward journey. The train came in and he boarded the last carriage, as he did every day. But at Michel-Ange Molitor, instead of getting out, he changed platforms and took the same line in the opposite direction. He went right through the Ranelagh stop. He got out at Franklin-Roosevelt.

It was the eleventh of May nineteen forty-seven. He was eleven years and two months old. He had just run away from home, 18, Rue de l'Assomption, in the sixteenth *arrondissement*; he wore a grey wool jacket with three buttons, a pair of navy shorts, brown shoes, blue woollen socks. He carried a satchel of imitation leather. All he possessed was twenty-three francs, and his only hope lay in selling his little stamp collection as quickly as he could.

He saw the woman behind the counter watching him and he stopped opening the gate. He did not move. He pressed himself against the tiled wall and waited.

A long time afterwards, the woman behind the counter came out to him.

You can't stay here you know, you're in the way, she said.

He said nothing. He did not look at her.

What are you doing here? she asked.

Nothing, he answered.

Where do you live? she enquired.

Ranelagh, he muttered.

Better go home to bed, she said.

Haven't got a ticket, he said.

She went to fetch him one, came back and held it out.

Haven't got any money, he said.

It doesn't matter, she said. It's a present. Now go home to bed.

He ran down to the platform.

A train arrived, it was almost empty; he got in. He sat down. The train left, the carriages shuddered and swayed. He found the noise of the métro rather reassuring.

At Trocadéro, he got out, not daring to go as far as Ranelagh. He changed and took the Mairie de Montreuil line. He got out at Alma-Marceau. He loitered on the platform for some time. He followed the zigzags made by the water-carts. He rummaged through the piles of tickets in the waste bins.

Later he sat down by the sweet machine. He watched the trains arrive. He tried to memorize the numbers written up over the leading carriages. He watched people arrive and leave.

Finally he got in the métro again, changed at Franklin-Roosevelt, and left by the Vincennes-Neuilly line, coming up at the Avenue des Champs-Élysées.

When Wednesday came round again, in the early afternoon, he took the métro as far as Pont de Sèvres, once more going back via Ranelagh—he huddled up in his seat—via Michel-Ange-Auteuil, and Michel-Ange-Molitor. At Pont de Sèvres, he crossed the Seine and went into the wood.

He walked and walked; occasionally he saw a gardener pruning a hedge, a man exercising his dog.

He left the main *allées*, and took smaller and smaller paths until he was beating his way through the bushes. At the top of a slight rise strewn with small stones and brambles, three trees, their trunks almost touching, formed a shelter, which would make a good camp. He cleared it carefully, digging out the brambles and weeds with his heels, piling up stones and gravel.

He sat down then against the largest of the three tree trunks. Later, with the sharp edge of a small stone, he made a large scratch in the bark of one of the three trees and, with various signs, marked out his way back. He no longer had a ticket to return to Franklin-Roosevelt. His card had been used twice. Timidly he asked the man punching the card to use the Thursday hole. He claimed he had made a mistake and forgotten to get off. The ticket-collector gave him a look and let him through.

He sat down on a green wooden bench and watched the merry-go-round again. The workmen had finished putting on the horses and the other rides and were fixing a big blue and orange tent made of strong canvas over the cone-shaped structure of the roof; it was attached to the top by a huge metal eyelet, and held at the base by long white canvas braids which one of the workmen, at the top of a double ladder, stood interminably plaiting, and which were being masked by a surround festooned with pieces in the shape of triangles.

Later he went for a little walk through the rock-gardens around the Grand Palais on the Seine side, among the artificial stone steps, the artificial arches, the artificial wooden bridge. He leaned over the pool where three tiny goldfish were swimming.

Later, in the gutter he found a piece of worked metal, a kind of bent copper pipe that had a valve with a spring on one end and was threaded at the other.

He stopped at the top of the steps, near the Montreuil exit. Once or twice he bent over the barrier and swung back and forth. Then he looked at the adverts.

He heard a train coming. People ran to get on. He realized they must be going to the theatre because they were wearing bow ties. He pulled the gate towards him and kept it open for them to go through.

Trains arrived. Passengers surged on, others got off, and everyone was in a hurry. He opened and closed the gate. Nobody said anything to him, no one said thank you. Some looked at him, perhaps they were surprised—an idea that occurred to him suddenly—to see such a well-dressed boy, and for a moment he wondered whether to hold out his hand.

He walked round the marionette theatre. He found a marble on the ground, an agate, a piece of worn white glass with a pigmentation of bubbles and shards, brightly decorated with a blue and yellow chain motif.

He leaned over the silent holes in the fountains, over the flowerless borders of the roundabout.

For a long time he watched the workmen assembling the merry-go-round. They were attaching two little cars, blue decorated with an orange sun, then some rather stylized horses, white, brown, and black, with spiky manes of blue or yellow, orange or green, and eyes that were made of two halves of wooden marbles embedded one inside the other, alternately blue and red.

Later he sat down and looked at what he had in his wallet: a school identity card, a métro ticket, a photo of his cousin at a fancy-dress ball with a dress sewn all over with shells, a photo of himself on the balcony in the Rue de l'Assomption.

He walked all around the traffic island, Avenue Matignon, Rue du Colisée, up as far as Saint-Philippe du Roule. It must be midday. People were queuing in front of the bread-shops. The cafés were full.

Later he walked slowly in the middle of a crowd rushing in all directions. Newspaper vendors were shouting: *Le Monde, France-Soir*. Clusters of people waited at the cross-roads, the bus stops, they were swallowed up in the mouth of the métro. Still later, when it was night time, he went up and down the Champs-Élysées, stopping at the doors of cinemas, looking at the windows of shops, slipping between the tables outside the cafés. Later he stopped for a long time next to the newspaper-seller at Franklin-Roosevelt who, under a canvas shelter lit by an oil lamp, was selling the latest editions of newspapers.

He confessed almost straight away. He told them what he was called. He gave his uncle's name, his telephone number, his address.

He looked at the policemen leaning over him, and wept.

Are you hungry? asked a policeman.

He did not answer.

Haven't you eaten anything?

He indicated that he had not.

They brought him a pâté sandwich, so big he had to make a great effort to tear at each mouthful. The bread was a little stale, the pâté tasted rather bitter. He was still crying and sniffing as he ate. He was trembling a little. Crumbs of pâté and bread fell onto the stained blotter.

Give him something to drink, said a voice.

A policeman came back, holding a bowl filled with water and handed it to him. He put his sandwich down on the blotter and grasped the bowl with both hands.

It was a huge, deep bowl, made of white china, the rim was chipped, the bottom stained with greyish streaks. He wet his lips in the water and drank.

Later the man who had brought him left. He was alone with the police, in front of the half-eaten sandwich, the white china bowl, the stained blotter, the inkwell and pads.

They indicated he should get up and go and sit somewhere else. He went to the back of the room, and sat on a wooden bench which ran along the whole wall. His hands on his knees, head bent, looking at the floor, he waited, full of shame and fear.

Later on his uncle and cousin arrived and took him off in the car.

When after twenty years he attempted to remember it all (when after twenty years I attempted to remember it all), everything at first was blurred and unclear.

Then, one by one, the details came back:

the marble, the bench, the bread roll;

the walk, the wood, the stones;

the merry-go-round, the marionettes;

the barrier;

the Rue de l'Assomption, the métro, the trains;

the comic, the man, the policemen;

the sandwich and the bowl, the large white china bowl, with the chipped rim, with the bottom covered with greyish streaks, from which he had drunk water (from which I had drunk water).

And he remained there a long time trembling, in front of the blank page (and I remained there a long time trembling, in front of the blank page).

May, nineteen sixty-five.

The House in the Place des Fêtes

Roger Grenier

'He was sorry he did not have several lives. Then he could have devoted one to her.'   John Dos Passos

During the war, Antoine Parrot had two girl-friends. One lived at Issy-les-Moulineaux behind the Parc des Exposi-tions; the other in the Place des Fêtes. He lived in a room in a hotel, whereas they each had a flat; which was why he went out with them only occasionally, preferring to go and see them at home. He usually went to Suzanne first, the one at Issy-les-Moulineaux. She lived on the sixth floor, in a block of council flats. The lift didn't work, because they were saving on electricity. You had to climb the stairs. Since Antoine Parrot did not normally give advance warning of his visits, he often found no one in. Suzanne, who was the boss's secretary in a firm, was frequently away on Saturdays and Sundays at her parents' house in the country, near

Vierzon. So Antoine Parrot, not much put out, would go back down the six floors, and make his way slowly to the métro. As he had to change, and the trains were infrequent, it took him a very long time to get to the Place des Fêtes.

It sometimes happened that he would again find no one in, and then there was nothing to be done but wander along the boulevards or go back to his room, in the district of Les Gobelins. But just seeing the Place des Fêtes and Dejanira's house was enough to make him happy.

Dejanira's house, on one corner of the square, had formerly been a little private school, an old, low building that dated from the beginning of the nineteenth century. It had belonged to the girl's grandparents and, after that, her parents. They were Greeks from Thrace, who had founded a school for the children of their fellow-countrymen. They had died some time ago, and Dejanira was left alone with her older sister, Antigone. In the house, which was too big, some rooms were still furnished with all the desks and benches, the dais and blackboard. On the faded wallpaper old photographs of lean, solemn people gazed into space, through the glass of the large picture frames. There was even a portrait of a bearded *papas*. Dejanira and Antigone were not well off and were managing on very little while continuing their studies. Antigone was twenty-six, just finishing medical school, and Dejanira, at nineteen, was in her first year studying law.

Antoine Parrot considered Antigone the prettier of the two, taller and slimmer. Dejanira had buck teeth like a rabbit. But she was the one he had got to know first and Antigone always received him rather distantly, as her sister's friend. There was something rather severe about her, owing to the fact that she was the elder and, after all, the head of the family. Besides, Antoine, a naturally modest man, when faced with two girls, chose the one he thought was not so beautiful. Dejanira was very lively and didn't take herself too seriously. She had large breasts, a well-rounded bottom, and laughed all the time with her rabbit teeth. Antoine was a head taller than her.

Sometimes it turned out that Antoine Parrot arrived at Issy-les-Moulineaux and the Place des Fêtes aware that his friends probably wouldn't be home. But, even when he found the door closed, he did not much mind. In life it is important to go through the motions, even though you may not actually do the thing itself.

One evening, after eating at Suzanne's, because she had brought back some food from a weekend at her parents' house, he stayed on after the curfew. In relations between men and women there always exists an unspoken code, a series of tacit conventions; these are both more precise and more charged with meaning than the spoken word, for people often talk in order to avoid saying anything, whereas this code always has some significance. In the code of the time, if a girl did not send you away before the curfew it meant that you would end up in bed with her. Since the outcome was certain, Antoine did not make a move immediately. Suzanne sat in a leather armchair, looking up at him out of half-closed eyelids while he held forth about the poetry of the Resistance, Éluard, and Aragon. At about one o'clock in the morning he leaned over the arm of the chair and gave her a kiss.

'I was wondering if you would dare,' she said. 'I've spent the whole evening trying to guess what time you would make up your mind.' The first hurdle over, he became more adventurous and pretended he had to persuade Suzanne to let him come to bed with her. She seemed to find this completely unexpected and not at all an attractive proposition. Eventually she lent him a pair of floral pyjamas which he found hard to get into, but thought he wouldn't be wearing for very long. She went to put some on as well. Once in bed, in the darkness, he discovered that her feet were like ice, and he offered to warm them up. Without more ado, she placed them on his, and the cold went right through him, momentarily quenching his desire. But you become accustomed to anything, and he started kissing and caressing her again. He unbuttoned her pyjama top and played with her breasts for a long time. But when he slid his hand further down, she kept her legs closed, and no amount of pleading, kissing, or caressing could make her open them.

After that he spent the night with Suzanne on several occasions. She slept in his arms, first offering him her mouth and breasts, unabashed by the feel of his masculinity, demanding its due, against her thighs or her belly. But she kept her legs tightly shut nevertheless. Finally one night she granted him what he was hoping for, but with bad grace, and almost making it seem as if nothing had happened.

She carried on going frequently to Vierzon. When she wasn't there, Antoine made his way to the Place des Fêtes. In the old house where everything was faded, except for Dejanira, he was welcomed with laughter, chatter, and the large black eyes of the young Greek girl with the rabbit teeth. Sometimes Antigone put in an appearance; she was rather cold towards him, but lovely to look at. When she went away, Antoine asked Dejanira: 'Hasn't your sister got a boyfriend?' All he got by way of an answer from Dejanira was a shrug.

The house smelled damp, like old country houses where the shutters have been closed for too long. In spite of her gaiety, Dejanira often spoke about her poverty. She had an old leather handbag, all discoloured, coming to pieces in several places. Talking of poverty, women can contrive to look smart on very little. But their handbags give them away. Dejanira thought Antoine, who had just finished his law degree and earned very little being articled to a solicitor, quite a wealthy man.

After the Allied landings in Normandy, the firm employing Suzanne closed down and the girl, not having any source of income, decided to go to her parents' house and await the Liberation. She asked Antoine if he could go with her as far as Vierzon, to help her carry her luggage. He took a day off. She had all manner of cases and bags and they had difficulty dragging them through the crowded métro, and the no less crowded train at the Gare d'Austerlitz.

Antoine stayed only a few hours in Sologne. He did not know what Suzanne had told her parents, but felt that they treated him more like a fiancé than a friend. He ate a large meal, the likes of which he had not eaten for some months. He went for a walk in the woods with Suzanne and they made love a little, standing against a tree. When it was time to go, Suzanne started to cry. Antoine told her the war would soon be over.

In Paris, life was punctuated by air-raid warnings, and then the métro came to a halt. But Antoine often went up to the Place des Fêtes. If he found something to eat he would bring it for the young Greek girls and would stay to supper with them. One day, when Dejanira was on her own peeling vegetables in the kitchen, wearing a blue apron that was too big for her, tied at the back, Antoine, feeling rather frivolous, undid her bow two or three times. Dejanira told him not to be silly and did it up again. When he undid it again, she turned round and started to fight him. A moment later and she was on the floor, on the old red tiles, brought down by Antoine. There was no animosity in their struggle. It was a game. It was not long before Antoine could not help feeling Dejanira's full, round breasts. As she allowed him, he began to kiss her. Her lips rounded, swelled tenderly, opened, hiding her buck teeth, and he encountered an agile tongue.

'Who taught you to kiss like that?' he demanded.

'I'm not a complete beginner,' Dejanira replied.

He continued his rapid conquest. He had imagined his hand would find a little fleece, with rebellious curls like a little urchin's unruly mop. Instead he found fronds of seaweed, she was moist and ready for love.

'You must be really uncomfortable on those tiles,' said Antoine.

He helped Dejanira up. She led the way into the nearby bedroom. The shutters were still closed. She got undressed in the half-light, laughing in embarrassment.

'It's the first time I've got undressed in front of a boy. It feels funny.'

She hopped around first on one leg and then the other, with her dark breasts, quivering slightly, looking as if they might burst. Her well-rounded little figure, with its curving silhouette, was charming and rather old-fashioned. The bed was a real old bed, very high. Dejanira climbed into it, and stretched out. Antoine tried to make love to her very gently. It hurt her a little, though she was more scared than hurt.

'Why did you choose me for your first time?' asked Antoine.

'Because . . . . That's my business.'

'It worries me a bit, because you are not the one I love. I think I love Suzanne.'

Dejanira pulled herself free of him, jumped out of bed, and put her clothes back on. Antoine started to explain.

'Shut up,' she said.

He got up as well, and hung around the house for a while, following Dejanira from room to room. But the sadness and hostility of the young girl, which he had no way of countering, made him take his leave. When he said goodbye, she did not return his kiss.

The next day he sent Dejanira a message,[1] asking her to phone. She called him at the end of the day, in the solicitor's office. He asked her how she was.

'Fine. I'm fine.'

'Can we meet?'

'Yes, but not at my house.'

'All right then, let's go and have a drink, in the Latin Quarter, or somewhere.'

---

[1] The French word is '*pneumatique*'. Letters were for many years sent by pneumatic tube in Paris and other cities.

They made a date for the following day, and met at the Mahieu. It was hot. Dejanira had put on a pleated navy skirt, a rather faded blouse, and across her shoulders she was carrying her old bag that was coming to pieces. She seemed to be in a bad mood. In order to keep the conversation going, Antoine Parrot talked about what he had been reading recently. He had discovered an extraordinary account in a magazine: 'The illustrious Thomas Wilson'. Dejanira asked him to lend her some books.

'Let's hop over to my place then, at Gobelins,' said Antoine.

They went on foot, by way of the Rue Gay-Lussac and the Rue Claude-Bernard. It was good to be out walking.

In the hotel lodgings, Antoine selected one or two books, and then made to kiss Dejanira. She would not give him her lips, and she fought him off. He plunged his hand down the front of her dress to take hold of her breasts, but she flung herself back so violently that her blouse with its rather worn material tore at the shoulder.

'That always happens, with you,' she said.

She began to heap hurtful remarks upon him. One thing she said was that considering he wanted to become a lawyer he was lacking the most basic understanding of human nature.

Antoine gave Dejanira a needle and thread. She took off her blouse, sat on the bed, and began to sew with tiny, careful stitches. Antoine watched her silently: the girl in her slip with straps that cut across her shoulders, the smooth, fine grain of her skin, the furrow between her breasts, all these combined to make a picture which was powerfully attractive to him. But at the same time, seeing her back bent over by the sewing, her air of sadness, and her humiliation in taking off her clothes, not to make love, but to repair a disaster, he felt as guilty as if he were the son of a banker who had tried to rape a working-class girl.

When she had finished her mending, Dejanira got up, and put her blouse back on again. As she buttoned herself up, Antoine had the overwhelming feeling that he was about to lose for ever the two breasts that had just vanished from his sight.

After that disastrous evening, Antoine did go back to the Place des Fêtes, but not so often. Dejanira and he had become just good friends once more. From time to time the girl would indicate, by some hurtful little remark, that she had not totally got over her bitterness and mistrust. She also asked him, always with a certain wounded irony, for news of Suzanne.

Paris was liberated. Antoine Parrot changed his job and became assistant to a well-known lawyer. He had a lot of work, and went even less frequently to the Place des Fêtes. Dejanira told him that he was becoming rather self-important and that he would have to be careful he did not get too smug. One day she announced that she had taken a lover, a tormented, idealistic student.

'I'm not in love with him. But I think I am very sensual. I can't do without it.'

Suzanne came back to Paris. Antoine went to meet her at the station. Since he loved her, he had a sense of disappointment when he saw her arrive on the platform. He had been thinking about her too much, and he scarcely recognized her. She felt it, and her smile of greeting froze on her lips. She said:

'If you don't like me any more, you can forget it.'

He protested. He felt as much to blame, in a way, as the day he had torn Dejanira's blouse. He took Suzanne's bags. He was not of an introspective nature or he would perhaps have realized that the bond that held him fast to Suzanne was not love, but fear. Nevertheless it was a bond, and it was easy to make mistakes. That night he stayed with her. He became accustomed to Suzanne again but, in spite of the love he thought he had for her, he never quite managed to forget the disappointment he had felt that moment when she got off the train.

A few weeks later, just as he was leaving his boss's office, Antoine Parrot was astonished to find Suzanne waiting for him on the pavement outside. It was the first time she had come to meet him after work. He hardly had time to kiss her before she said: 'Supposing we get married?'

To make preparations for the wedding, Suzanne began to return to Vierzon quite often. She brought back bits of furniture and crockery. Her mother was getting her trousseau ready. Antoine, full of enthusiasm for his new job, often had too much work to go with her, and remained behind in Paris.

One Sunday, after he had finished reading up on a case, he went to the Place des Fêtes. The house was as charming as ever, and he loved that silly little flutter of excitement when he rang the bell, not knowing if the door would be opened or if Dejanira would already have gone out. This time the young Greek girl was there with her sister, the pretty Antigone. Now that Antigone had passed the exam for her internship, she left late in the afternoon for the hospital. Antoine said he was going to marry Suzanne. Dejanira said: 'I knew from the start that you would.'

When it was time to leave, he almost had his hand on the handle of the door when Dejanira gave him a teasing look and declared: 'I've so wanted to kiss you today!'

'That's not a problem!'

He took her face in his hands and began kissing her at length. Without tearing anything this time, he undid her blouse and pulled out her breasts.

'Oh yes, kiss my breasts again,' said Dejanira. But that was all he did that day in the hallway of the old house, because she said she was sorry, it was one of those days.

Antoine and Suzanne got married. Antoine left his lodgings and moved to the flat in Issy-les-Moulineaux. After the wedding he went back one more time to see Dejanira. Again she seemed to him withdrawn, slightly contemptuous of him. She told him that the student who had been her lover had just killed himself with a bullet through the heart. He was terribly depressed and was feeling rejected by the world. The way she said it made Antoine feel ashamed of his good position in society, with a wedded wife, a flat, and a job with excellent prospects. The student had left his private diary to Dejanira.

'I'd lend it you,' she told Antoine, 'but I don't trust you. You know too many journalists. You would be quite capable of handing it over to them.'

Dejanira was harsh and resentful towards him, but she did not seem to be in despair at the death of her lover, which was the main thing.

On another occasion, Antoine met her on the boulevard in front of the Palais de Justice. He walked a little way with her, as far as the Place Saint-Michel.

'How is Suzanne? Still being nasty to you?' she asked him.

Wherever could she have got that from?

A few months later, while Suzanne had gone to Vierzon for a few days, Antoine had a sudden urge to go to the Place des Fêtes. At the end of the long métro journey, there was the escalator again, and immediately you were out in the open air—in another world, it seemed. Dejanira wasn't there and he left a note in the letter-box to ask the girl to phone him.

When he went back down into the métro, the travellers' faces seemed to him to be either stupid or malevolent. None seemed in any doubt about their own importance or right to take up a certain space or breathe in their neighbour's air. None seemed to have a kindly or compassionate look for anyone else. Each of them, stony-faced or hostile, was wrapped up in his own thoughts. Antoine wanted to cry like a baby. The next day Dejanira called him.

'I'm always coming to your place,' he said. 'Why not come to mine for a change? Come and have some lunch with me.'

When he opened the door to her, he saw that she was wearing a hat that was completely ridiculous as well as ugly. She was smiling, with all her buck teeth showing. Poor Dejanira! Dressing up didn't suit her.

He made her take off her hat and coat and gave her a glass of wine. Then, while she went round the room, inspecting each piece of furniture, each ornament, he went into the kitchen to prepare lunch: steak and spaghetti. After they had eaten, he left her again, to go and make some coffee. She lit a cigarette.

When she went into the kitchen the water was boiling.

'How is it going?' she asked.

Antoine poured boiling water into the coffee pot and put the saucepan back on the stove. Dejanira flung herself into his arms. It was a real leap, at least Antoine had the impression she had leapt and that he had caught her in mid-flight. Between two kisses she said to him: 'I don't know what it is, but there is definitely something between us, something...'

'You are right,' Antoine agreed.

They moved to the other room and Dejanira went and lay on the conjugal bed.

For a long time after that Antoine did not have an opportunity to see Dejanira. Some days he wanted to see her a lot, but in fact did not have time, or else the door at the Place des Fêtes was shut. They went their separate ways, as they say. Dejanira finished her studies, and Antoine found out that she was married and had gone to live in the country, somewhere in the Sarthe or the Mayenne.

We all have our little pilgrimages, our shrines. Once every five years, perhaps, Antoine chances to be in the area of the Place des Fêtes. Entire neighbourhoods near there have been pulled down. Yet the old school which was Dejanira's house remains standing. Antoine would have preferred it to be demolished along with the rest. But there it is, looking rather squashed up now on the corner of the street; it seems as if you would only have to ring the doorbell. And he has to make a determined effort not to go and ring. Everything is so unchanged. Behind the window on the right, behind the curtains, is the room where he undid Dejanira's blouse and stroked her breasts when she was nineteen. When he goes away it takes him at least the whole journey across Paris before he can forget the injustice time has done to him, a far greater injustice than all those he pleads against at the Palais de Justice. But then, Paris is huge, and he doesn't think about the house very often, not until the next time. Is it still standing? Did they finally knock it down? He doesn't know whether to hope that he will, or hope that he will not, see it again, the day he returns to the Place des Fêtes.

The Joyful Death of Fassola

Andrée Chedid

Fassola woke and moved a little. Not too painful, not too scary. Her arms and hands tingled and her head felt rather muzzy. But the coffin lid gave easily at her push, with only the faintest squeak. The fine dusting of soil which had been thrown on to it, along with one or two flowers which had so far not had time to wither, slid off the sides with a small swooshing sound.

The tomb was not yet sealed. The burial had taken place in a hurry the day before, and it had not been possible to finish things off properly.

It was the middle of August. Sympathetic neighbours had taken charge of arrangements for the undertakers and the funeral, there being an almost total absence of her few relatives and friends. Since it was the day before they went on holiday and also extremely hot, they hurried the process along and cut short the funeral service, with the consent of a distant nephew they managed to contact by phone.

The 'proper, definitive' tombstone was to be finished in the next few days. It occurred to Fassola that she did not much care for those two adjectives. They had such a ring of finality about them. On the other hand she was delighted about the hastiness, which would leave things unresolved and give her a chance to poke her nose outside and enjoy a completely novel and untoward experience.

She was quite convinced she must be dead. Everything around her confirmed that impression. But was she still the person who encompassed all those thoughts and feelings she recognized as hers? With fingers that were rather stiff she explored her breasts, her hips, her thighs; she rediscovered her familiar contours and felt a sense of relief.

She allowed the palms of her hands, then, to travel over her face, locating the slightly snub nose and protruding grey wart at the corner of her left eye, which she insisted on calling her 'beauty spot'. She ascertained that her hair, which was fairly short, felt as thick as usual, but damp and untidy as a result of this first night without air.

Lastly she recognized the dress she had been wearing two days before, a loosely cut floral orange print, and remembered her taste for bright colours. She also had on her comfortable beige canvas shoes; they were worn at the toes and several years old.

Daylight came with a fitful breeze, swaying like a little boat above the grave.

Fassola sat up, stretched, and hauled herself into the daylight. Reaching the top she perched on the edge of her tomb and glanced all around her. There was no one about. She gave her clothes a shake, tapped her feet on the ground to rid herself of the remaining dust. She had not dallied long enough in the other world to lose her self-confidence, and she was reassured by the thought that she looked quite normal still and would not strike terror into the living.

At the same time she harboured a feeling of resentment towards death, with whom she had enjoyed a cordial, even chummy, relationship until now. Why should death, pre-empting the plans they had made together and rejecting what Fassola considered to be a tacit understanding, come for her a year before the allotted time, in the middle of her sixty-fourth year?

That extra year would have been enough for her to achieve her goals, financial and otherwise. She had married at eighteen, divorced almost immediately, brought up a son who had gone off to live in Australia, and ended up running a small business at the age of fifty. Having been an account-ant for some years in the clothes business, she had, through force of habit, calculated everything down to the last centime and made up her mind that at sixty-five, having made the most of her earnings, she would bow out while still in good health: 'Bye, everyone!'

What was she to make of this impulsive action on the part of her untrustworthy partner? She had imagined death to be more flexible, more malleable, rather more like life was! But now death had struck her down blindly, pig-headedly, mechanically, as if on a sudden change of heart. Fassola was quite contentedly sitting at dinner with friends when, without any warning, her pulse missed a beat and suddenly stopped.

There was nothing to be done, and she just had to accept it. But what happened so quickly after that? Had the Reaper been stricken with remorse a bit late in the day? Or was it her own life-force breathing what remained of her spirit into a dormant body?

Suspecting that this would only be a short leave of absence, Fassola decided to have a last look at the town, at things, at people. Her eyes were all the brighter because she knew they came from 'elsewhere'; were, so to speak, 'on loan'.

Fassola could not remember anything about the world beyond, in which she had been immersed for such a short time. Not a thing. Death was not how some imagined it. It wasn't a chamber of horrors, nor a sweetly scented garden. No terrifying visions had appeared, but nor did she see those poetic, radiant landscapes sometimes described so ecstatically by people who have been in a coma and come back to life again. She had experienced none of these sensations, of that she was positive. She had quite simply tumbled into death as you might fall into a hole—and then climbed out again. Either way she felt nothing. Nothing.

Quietly she recalled her grandfather's death. She was ten at the time; he was over eighty. He had died in his sleep, during one of his peaceful nights, tucked up snugly between the smooth sheets.

On the other hand the second time she came across death it was unbearable. Her eldest brother Jacques was sixteen. That afternoon on his way home from school he crashed head-first into the back of a lorry that had braked abruptly. His agony lasted a week. They told lies to his little sister but she managed to enter the hospital without anyone knowing and get into his room. For more than an hour she gazed, petrified, upon his beloved, tortured face; he was already in another world. It took her ages to get over it; for a long time she loathed death.

'Your brother is in Paradise. He was a saint, he said his prayers every day. We shall see him again in the other world . . . .'

None of these words of consolation found any favour with Fassola. The fact of the matter was that Jacques had gone for ever. She preferred to face up to it. But after such annihilation as this, what meaning was there in life?

The notion of the Promised Land, the truth of which was asserted by believers everywhere, and of every faith, only made her more antagonistic. So there were barriers, enclaves, frontiers even beyond our own! This Deity they all claimed as theirs seemed to her to be a guardian of the tombs, a surly keeper of accounts fanning the flames of dissension, on the look-out for victims.

However, the idea of a more vast, more merciful God was also beginning to emerge. She did not totally exclude this God; but, imagining Him to be of an essence so fundamentally different from that of men, she preferred, in the face of these ethereal visions, to view matters in a more prosaic light.

Life took its course. Gradually Fassola grew closer to death and recognized how harmless it was. Death played the part assigned to her by nature, ensuring, through successive exterminations, the survival of the species. Death glorified life, after her own fashion.

From then on, Fassola treated death as a daily companion. A companion who helped her, as she lived her life, to distinguish inessentials from the essential, the branches from the trunk of the tree, the waves from the ocean.

Sitting on her tombstone, Fassola became calm again. At the thought of all those people lying under their beds of earth, all these new companions she was about to abandon for an hour or two, she gave a brief wave, as if to say: 'I'll be back, I'll be back!', before making her way towards the deserted avenue.

She was delighted by this respite, and made up her mind she would fill her eyes, nose, ears, full of this noisy city, which she would soon have to leave for ever.

Fassola resolved not to go back to her little flat, but to leave it to its future occupants. Instead she would enjoy to the full the whole of existence, all the things that would go on existing without her, everything she had always enjoyed.

The end had come in a brutal manner; she had not had time to share out her favourite possessions among her nearest and dearest. Not that there were many of them, nor worth very much. But they meant something to her. A piece of lava, a smooth, black stone, a shell in the shape of a cave, each object discovered in unforgettable circumstances. A large pen with a plume, a big bluish bowl she used for the sort of food she enjoyed: steaming hot and plenty of it. She had always been suspicious of possessions, for didn't they threaten to possess you, to devour you instead?

Fanciful yet practical, dreamy but organized, and passionate in her quiet way, Fassola, as always, handled all these contradictions cheerfully and expertly. She always welcomed the dawn each day as if it were a special gift. She was afraid of only one thing—that by the time she was old she would not have had enough of it!

It looked as if it would be a beautiful day. The haze hung brooding over a flaxen sky. In order to get rid of the slight tingling in her back, her arms, her legs, Fassola raised herself on tiptoe several times in succession; the solid feel to her ankles and knees afforded her real satisfaction.

A sparrow, leaving its flock in full flight, came hopping around her; then perched on her shoulder, twittering. Feeling the little claws of the bird through the cloth, she made her way with a light heart into the central avenue, where the tombs were grander and spaced further apart. Several times, as she turned to look at her own among the others, underneath a young sapling, she congratulated herself upon her choice. She left the cemetery by a side entrance where the iron gate had been left half open. Then she went into the Boulevard Edgar Quinet.

A dog ran up, through her legs, taking no notice of her. She did not feel him bump or rub against her at all. A man in a hurry did the same; Fassola jumped to one side to get out of the way, apologized out loud, but the passer-by seemed neither to hear nor see her. Feeling rather peculiar, she decided to go to the nearest café to fortify herself.

There she sat down among the other customers, at the counter. She gave her order—coffee and croissants—in a clear, friendly voice. No one batted an eyelid.

She turned first to one person and then another, trying to attract their attention. Her soundless words, her insubstantial gestures floated away into the air. At length she realized that her body existed for her, and only for her. She felt as if she might collapse, her head was spinning and her spirits sank. It was the sight of the sparrow hopping up and down on the pavement, waiting for her to come out, that happily made her regain her composure.

She nibbled bits of croissant here and there, and drained what was left in the coffee cups. Her sensations had not yet become dulled; she felt comforted by the drinks and the food. But gradually, trammelled by her own movements and imprisoned by her lonely words which came echoing back at her, she felt bitterly deprived of the sharing and the reciprocity which is the very stuff of life. Tears came to her eyes. She ran out to the bird again.

He recognized her and made joyful little sounds, then flew up on to her shoulder once more.

Fassola walked to the bus-stop and got on the first bus, while the sparrow took its place on the roof. She found a seat near the window and sat down without disturbing anyone. She never tired of the familiar sights of Paris.

She drank them in with her eyes, her face pressed to the glass.

While she was invisible, she was free, absolutely free. But her freedom seemed cold as ice, no use to her. With no one to talk to, even the city lost its splendour. Trees looked stiff, faces seemed lifeless.

After an hour she found herself once more in the Boulevard Edgar Quinet:

'Anyone for the cemetery?' shouted the driver in a joky voice.

Knowing that she would not be noticed, she shouted: 'Yes, me, Fassola!' It was just so that she could hear the sound of her own name inside her own heart.

As she got off the steps of the bus she was relieved to feel the delicate claw of the little sparrow on her shoulder, and then the softness of his down against her neck.

In the cemetery Fassola saw three gravediggers carrying their spades and rakes. They were making their way towards her grave. She made haste so as to get there before them.

Death had been right not to take her oath too seriously. She loved people, loved life too much. She would never have willingly made up her mind to take her leave of everything. The Reaper must surely have decided to capture her as a considerate act towards an old friend, thus removing all uncertainty, as well as the wear and tear of old age?

Fassola got down into the grave, stretched out in her housing of oak, and calmly pulled down the lid, in profound relief at this unceremonious leave-taking.

The distraught sparrow attempted to get in with her. He flapped his wings furiously, pecked at the wood of the coffin with his beak, and began to chatter to let her know he was there.

Fassola was so moved that she felt once more a part of life.

She tapped with a crooked finger several times on the inside to make the bird go away. She had to break off this communication, stifle this feeling that was holding her back to no purpose.

The bird gave up only when the first spadefuls of earth were emptied on to the coffin.

Then he flew away.

And at the same moment Fassola herself took flight.

The Man with the Collecting-Box

Didier Daeninckx

He came out of the doorway almost opposite the Caveau de la Huchette.[1] Behind the glass display windows, photos of Memphis Slim veered to and fro like gondolas. The street was no better; it twisted and turned every which way, like a serpent on the attack.

He had to shut his eyes against the sun. He was forced to lean against the wall so that he would not fall over. His head was spinning as fast as ever. He took slow, deep breaths. His heart steadied and the sickness in his stomach eased a little. He set off once more, head down, shoulders hunched, until he reached the Rue Saint-Jacques, and then turned right

---

[1] The famous jazz club in the Rue de la Huchette at the bottom right of the Boulevard Saint-Michel.

towards the Taverne. He was preparing to cross the road when someone put his hand on his shoulder.

'Where you off to, mate?'

The voice was not friendly. He raised his eyes. A helmeted policeman, his eyes shaded by protective glasses, stood in front of him.

'I'm going for a drink. That against the law?'

The policeman gave him a violent push backwards. He staggered and fell with a thud on to the pavement. Passers-by avoided him, without a word. Instead of getting back up, he slithered along on his hands and feet to the wall, and sat there with his back against it. Police stretched out all along the street and blocked off the bridge to the Île de la Cité as well. The café tables outside the Taverne were deserted and he could make out the shapes of waiters standing around with nothing to do. The noise up near the Sorbonne became louder. A dark mass of people formed in the middle of the road. The police regrouped and a sergeant gave the order to charge. Alain waited for them to pass the crossroads of the Boulevard Saint-Germain before getting up and hobbling over to the Taverne. He sat down in the room at the back near the juke-box, at one of the tables served by Jean-Mi. The waiter came forward and wiped the table mechanically.

'What do you want? This is really not the moment to . . .'

He put his own hand over the hand flicking the cloth. His lips scarcely moved.

'I'm the one who decides when it's the right moment.'

Jean-Mi tried to pull his hand free. 'Let me go . . . . You can see how many cops there are about. It's very risky.'

'I'm desperate, I've got the cash on me. Bring me a coffee and we'll meet in the gents, as usual.'

He drank his coffee and the room filled up with students and anxious passers-by keeping out of any trouble. He saw Jean-Mi put his tray down behind the bar, and got up. Somebody was bawling into the taxi-phone wedged under the stairs. The waiter stood at the porcelain and undid his zip. The other made a show of washing his hands, looking at the waiter in the mirror.

'So, Jean-Mi, you making things difficult?'

'Where've you been, Alain? We've been under siege round here for the last week. There are more cops between Saint-Michel and the Odéon than tourists at the foot of the Eiffel Tower. Nobody's got anything any more, it's too risky.'

Alain undid his old winter coat, felt in the torn lining, and drew out a brown paper bag with a pattern of green fruit printed on it.

'Twenty bags . . .[2] You're not going to turn up your nose at that?'

Jean-Mi pressed the chrome button on the urinal with the palm of his hand. As the water gurgled, he shrugged.

---

[2] A '*sac*' in this context means ten francs.

'Even if you do manage to find somebody, you'll have to keep out of the way. I heard them say they weren't selling it for less than four hundred francs a shot . . . And that was yesterday.'

That evening, when the cramps became too acute, Alain tried to dull them with cognac. For the last fortnight he had been staying at Beaubourg in what had once been a brothel and was now a squat for the tramps around Saint-Merri. The squat looked out on to the huge dilapidated square, used as a car park by the traders who came to load up at Les Halles. Before getting completely sodden with drink he stuffed the remaining notes in his pants. The alcohol reached his nerve-ends in the small hours. The next evening he obtained the number of a dealer selling cheap dope in the Luxembourg area. He went up the Boulevard Saint-Michel again, walking in the middle of the road between the piles of torn-up paving stones, the torn-down trees, and the burnt-out shells of cars. The dealer was on his own, eating a hamburger at the table nearest the entrance to the Wimpy. Alain came and sat down on his left, as arranged. He waved the salt-cellar placed in front of him on the table.

'Got the salt and pepper?'

The man retrieved a slice of onion which had just fallen onto the formica top.

'Show me what you've got first. I don't let it go for less

than three-fifty. If everything's in order we'll get the goods later.'

Alain banged the salt-pot down on the table.

'You crazy? That's a swindle.'

'If you really want it, you'll pay. I'm one of the very few with some still left. But you'd better get a move on.'

Sunday 12 May 1968 was one of the worst days of his life. He spent it in the squat in the Rue Saint-Martin, numbing his senses with alcohol and valium. He emerged on Monday afternoon and traipsed around the area of the Taverne and the Wimpy without meeting anybody. He was on the Pont Saint-Michel when the head of the demonstration coming from République began to darken the Boulevard du Palais. A car with a loud-hailer took up its position level with the Sainte-Chapelle and their driver waited for the first cohort of demonstrators before he plugged in the speakers.

'As a tribute to our comrades who fell on the barricades, we ask you to proceed quietly down the Boulevard Saint-Michel.'

Waves of quiet, one after another, spread through the Quartier Latin. Alain watched, without really understanding what was happening. Suddenly a girl with curly hair was standing in front of him, smiling. He stared at her uncomprehendingly. Then he heard the chink of coins and his eyes fell on the collecting-box which she was holding out and rattling at him. He read the label stuck on the cylindrical tin: 'For the Victims of Police Violence'.

He put his hand in his pocket, felt the ridge of a one-franc coin and pushed it through the slit. The girl thanked him and, one-by-one, asked all the other people standing round. Everybody put in a coin; he even saw some people stuff a note in the tin, without giving it a second thought.

On Tuesday morning, Alain spent his last few francs on a collecting-box, which an obsequious shopkeeper wrapped up as though it were a present from a poor man to his priest. The hitch-hiker from Holland who had fetched up in his room the night before had moved on and Alain wrote out his message in a careful hand: 'In Aid of the Injured Students'.

On the morning of 15 May he scoured the area around the occupied Sorbonne without achieving the hoped-for success. From time to time a generous passer-by would put in a reluctant coin, often with some suspicion. Not a single note. At noon Alain went to the Salvation Army in the Rue de Rome. When he had had his shower and his haircut, a woman in uniform took him to the bottom of the small stone steps. She ushered him into a cloakroom which stank of mothballs, and piled some neatly folded clothes into his arms. He inherited a pair of jeans and a sweater which made him look ten years younger. In the afternoon on the Boul' Mich' he was collecting outside a tobacconist's. In the ensuing two weeks you could see him everywhere. He was with the pickets on strike in the occupied stations, near the entrance to the métro, in the queues at the service-stations which had run out of petrol . . . . Everywhere he met with an enthusiastic reception. He never went out without his collecting-box wrapped up in a plastic bag, and he would unwrap it at the first demonstration, the first gathering of people he happened to come across. In the evenings in his broken-down squat in the old brothel he piled up the coins in tens or twenties according to colour, and rolled them up in strips of paper cut from *Le Parisien Libéré*.

He hit the jackpot on 18 May when the students went down in a procession to Billancourt. Charléty, on the other hand, was a dead loss, from his point of view.

The pusher at the Wimpy didn't accept coins, so he had to travel right across Paris to find a bank where the red flag was not flying. At the end of the month, after the CGT[3] demo from Bastille to Saint-Lazare, when he made 758 francs, he had a glass of wine outside the Taverne. Jean-Mi came to say hello.

'You still on the look-out?'

By way of an answer, Alain's eyes closed. The waiter went on: 'You see the guy over there.' He made an almost imperceptible gesture towards a man drinking beer, a sort

---

[3] The Confédération Générale du Travail, one of the largest French trade unions.

of a clown with prominent eyebrows, a dark-green dyed moustache, and very thick, black, shoulder-length hair.

'Which one? Medrano?'[4]

'Don't be fooled by his looks. He knows how to get some first-class stuff. Some LSD. Apparently if you haven't tried that you haven't tried anything. Do you want to be introduced?'

A moment later and Alain had arranged to meet the man with the moustache's exclusive supplier, at an address in the eighteenth *arrondissement* in the Avenue George V. He had to say he was from Mandala.

He went there on the last Friday in May. The collecting-box was in his bag, as usual. He was just about to turn into the avenue when a great clamour brought him up short. There was a demo spreading right across the Champs-Élysées, going up. He had never seen such an impressive one. Grasping his collecting-box, he hurried towards the procession, chanting: 'In Aid of the Injured Students, In Aid of the Injured Students.'

The first block of demonstrators opened up and immediately closed round him. A paratrooper in fatigues, red beret cocked over one ear, chest covered in medals, accosted him. Alain caught sight of a small printed sign waving above them: 'Organization of Former Combatants of Dien Bien Phu.'

---

[4] The owner of the famous Medrano circus always sported a large moustache on the posters.

His eyes met the cold flash of a bayonet. An injection of deadly steel. His last shout was drowned out by a thousand voices of a French nation once more recovering its identity:

'Renault back to work,

Commies back to Moscow . . .

Renault back to work,

Commies back to Moscow . . .'

Rue du Commerce

Jacques Réda

Some citadels, time-honoured by tradition, are impregnable. If you don't count the occasional markets (on Sundays one of the prettiest, largely because of its situation, stretches north from the overground métro), then you might say that there are three principal shrines to commerce in the fifteenth *arrondissement*. These are: part of the Rue Saint-Charles, between the Rue de la Convention and the Place Charles-Michels; the crossroads of Cambronne-Lecourbe; and the Rue du Commerce, which well deserves its name.

I should explain that by 'commerce', I do not mean a simple row of shops, of which you may find a goodly selection in other thoroughfares like the Rue du Vaugirard; in those streets an excessive amount of luxury goods, and especially clothing, exists side by side with establishments that guarantee the supply to one section of the *quartier* of bread, wine, vegetables, milk products, woollen goods, aspirin, nails, and newspapers. No, I am talking here about the dense concentration of shops dedicated to satisfying the basic necessities of life, where competition between the different spheres surfaces merely as a secondary phenomenon. Here, if you come across several cheese merchants, several butchers very close to one another, you get the impression that, far from being rivals, which would be to the customer's disadvantage, they are working together in solidarity to put the necessary riches into circulation. It is the manifestation of an abundance that is a real tonic to behold; they are not displaying this affluence just for the sake of it, but because it has its own function and *raison d'être*. Here the scourge of elementary economic balance scarcely tips the scales either way: supply is modestly adjusted to the demand it creates, which in turn—invariably prudent and circumspect—always regulates any possible excesses.

For several hundred metres, the Rue du Commerce thus offers everything a person might be supposed to require if he arrived naked and hungry (but with a wallet of course) from the Avenue de la Motte-Picquet or from the Rue de l'Abbé-Groult. In less than an hour that person could be shod, clothed, and replete, either by separate purchases at the desired specialist shops, or by doing his shopping all together in what is nowadays called a '*grande surface*'.[1] Stores like these have proliferated far and wide round even the smallest of towns, and now occupy countless strategic points within Paris itself. Yet they have never succeeded in ousting the local idea of buying and selling, which does accord with a certain way of seeing and feeling. The Rue Cler and the Rue Lévis, for instance, hold firmly to that tradition. And so, equally, does the Rue du Commerce, where the only two stores belonging to large firms are mouldering away quite lamentably. Yet one of them set itself up like a fortress right at the crossroads on the corner of the Boulevard de Grenelle, its architecture a vague hotchpotch of Art Nouveau, transatlantic steamship, and the Maginot Line. It might as well not have bothered. You would think the tide of desires surrounding it must have gone out, and that its shop window displays, looking out on to a sandy desert, cannot have altered since 1937.

Towards the other end of the street, the second of these two stores, under its abstract neon lighting, is in its death-throes. In Prague and Budapest I have visited such necropolises, made an inventory of what is on their almost bare shelves in full view of sad, suspicious shopgirls, and, because I was sorry for them, bought toys made out of tin which fell

---

[1]   A large shop, nowadays usually a supermarket or hypermarket.

to pieces in my suitcase, or ethnic blouses which I never even dared give anyone. There is an obvious capitalist opulence very different from the poverty of these state firms. But the one resembles the other in that everything in them appears to be artificial or unfit for sale, as well as in the dismal faces of their customers underneath the ghastly lighting.

The conflicting nature of these two ages and philosophies of commerce is best illustrated if you stop, a few dozen yards away from the aforementioned fortress, under the huge painted signs that hang above an ancient creamery, firmly binding the customer to the deeply pastoral, maternal origins of his desires. They have trees, streams, blue hills and meadows, ruminating cows, several lively goats, and a lovely farmer's wife who, in one arm, clasps her baby to her breast, and, in the other, carries a pail overflowing with energy-giving milk.

Coming back to our hypothetical person, nothing, then, would be easier for him than to acquire, in addition to the necessaries and a slab of butter, some earplugs, a watch, an umbrella, a few carnations, a French translation of the *Aeneid*, some glasses to re-read it, a travel bag even, should he be hoping to continue his journey as far as the Antipodes, for the aerodrome at Les Invalides is only four stops away on the métro. Perhaps not before lighting a candle to Saint-Jean-Baptiste-de-Grenelle in recognition of so many blessings. For God Himself, in fact, has a shop at the end of this street, and the gentle arcades of the church with the slightly Siamese-looking tower are just the place for some busy little second-hand stalls: here you can buy indulgences and sell off your old sins, come to a private agreement with the Virgin or Saint Antony, put your self-esteem in hock to a loan of liquid Grace, all too swiftly squandered.

Does this go against all mysticism? I'm not sure. Let us wait for the moment when the church in its turn gives vent to a sonorous display and from the top of the belltower pours forth ripe fruits into a sky half of which is already blue like a crypt, and half of which is burning with the fire of the angels. One after the other the darting, wavering flames of the huge starry brasier leap into the air; you can hear the crackling; the feeling that there is a short respite, or that something dramatic is about to occur, draws everyone who has been absorbed by the busyness of shopping out into the open:

> The absent, the abandoned,
> All those by their own
> Bitter selves unfairly
> Shut in, the drunk, the insane,
>
> History's reformers,
> The soapbox preachers whose
> Suddenly lifted fists
> Utter a loud '*J'accuse!*'

And the indifferent and those
Life dumbly terrifies
And some who are ashamed
Of crimes they only dreamed

Into the joyous din
Of crowds they are taken up.
It pleases them to idle
A while in the baker's shop

And when everything closes down
On evenings hot as hell
They are the city's hairdressers'
Only clientele

To talk about the times
That will not come again
While measures of the angelus
Break on the terrain

And stir the ghosts to walk
Towards childhoods that never were
And open hardened hearts
To pity harbouring there.

Sometimes a fire-engine from the Violet barracks, its spasmodic siren mingling with the hiccoughing undulations of the bells, brings all this excitement to fever-pitch, though it is held in check by an incoming tide of silence and inactivity. Then, from one of the establishments[2] which maintain

---

[2] Such as the Café du Commerce, established in 1921 and still an imposing presence in this street.

the dignity of popular restauration in Paris (veal's head, napkin rings, mirrors encompassing infinity), a waiter comes out onto the pavement for a second. Draped like an officiating priest in his long apron, he no doubt also believes that something is about to happen, some grandiose bartering operation between the horizon drowning in light and the people ready to hold out their hands; some apotheosis of the shop fronts gleaming with ironmongery and victuals. But it is only a passing moment. Already the metal shutters are coming down, bending the shadows; groups of fascinated onlookers disperse.

At the corner of the Rue Lakanal, someone fleeing like a thief with the last loaf of bread knocks into an old lady, balanced by her bags, doing some late shopping, and she is left swaying unsteadily on her feet. On the opposite side, the square, with its bandstand, trees, and little republican building, is as dark and distant as one of those villages where you end up exactly as night falls, as a result of all the disastrous wrong turnings taken on roads without signposts. And after a detour by way of the dark Rue des Écoliers, the now deserted Rue du Commerce is scarcely recognizable; it is artificial, like the painted street of a stage-set in which you are yourself afraid of being only a painting, with your shopping list lying forgotten in your pocket.

Plan of Occupancy

Jean Echenoz

Since everything—the mother, the furniture, and the photographs of the mother—had gone up in flames, Fabre and their son Paul had a lot to attend to immediately: all that ash and being in mourning, moving house and rushing around department stores, rebuilding their life. Fabre, rather too hastily, found something a bit smaller, a small flat with a sitting room that doubled as a bedroom. It was in the shadow of a brick chimney you could tell the time by, but it did have the advantage of being quite close to the Quai de Valmy.

In the evening when supper was over, sometimes even as soon as it had begun, Fabre talked to Paul about his, Paul's, mother. As they no longer possessed any likeness of Sylvie

Fabre he kept on trying to conjure her up, in ever more exact detail. The slightest imprecision threatened to deflate the holograms that sprang up in the middle of the kitchen. It can't be done, Fabre would sigh, putting his hand to his head and covering his eyes, and he would fall asleep in despair. It was often left to Paul to pull out the sofa and turn the room into a bedroom.

On Sundays and sometimes on Thursdays they went down to the Quai de Valmy, via the Rue Marseille or the Rue Dieu, to see Sylvie Fabre. She smiled down upon them in her fifteen metres of blue dress, holding out to them a bottle of Piver perfume by Forvil. The iron bars of a little window made a hole in her side. That was the only representation there was of her.

Flers, the artist, had painted her on the side of a block of flats almost at the end of the street. This building, in a better state of repair than the creaky old buildings that huddled up against it as though terrified at the prospect of their imminent demise, was not so wide, but more solid. Since it lacked a canopy, the name of the sculptor-architect, Wagner, was carved on a cartouche up in the right-hand corner of the lavishly decorated porch. And the wall on which Flers the artist and his team had toiled away at the full-length portrait of Sylvie Fabre overhung a small, rudimentary strip of grass, a kind of square without any trimmings, whose only function was to mark the end of the street.

Sylvie had agreed to pose, after being picked out by Flers and pressed by Fabre. She had not relished the experience. That was three years before Paul was born and so, as far as he was concerned, this wall belonged to a previous existence. Fabre was agitated by the sight, sometimes excited, sometimes reduced to tears. Just look at your mother! Quite often he would make a scene and start cursing the place where the portrait was, and his angry words would come echoing back at him. Paul had to calm his father down as soon as a small crowd threatened to gather.

Later on, Paul, now no longer even on speaking terms with his father, fell into a more flexible pattern of visiting his mother, two or three times a month, not counting the times he happened to pass that way. When they first started demolishing the crumbling old block abutting on to the Wagner building, he had almost telephoned his father from a call-box within Sylvie Fabre's field of vision. It remained there in isolation, like a beacon beside the canal. The restored façade, by the contrast it made, caused a sheen and unsuspected subtleties of shading to appear on the blue dress. It was a beautiful dress, extremely low-cut; she was a real mother. The old building was replaced by a smart modern one done out in white tiles, furbished with little curved balconies, while the other side of the Wagner building was fortunately still protected by the strip of grass at Sylvie's feet which made an extra little lawn.

Whether by accident or design, the site was allowed to deteriorate. It became more and more uncommon to find anything green in the brown residues around the mud, through which iron spikes poked menacingly, like the claws of tetanus itself stretching out to grab at passers-by. Anyone passing through these places will find them offensive. He will go out of his way to avoid areas so completely cut off from the world of chlorophyll. He will no longer send his offspring in that direction, will not walk that way any more when he exercises his dogs. And one morning, seeing they have been fenced off, he coldly approves this process of quarantining without ever questioning the reason for it. He is indifferent, concerned only with his own affairs.

With the passage of time the fencing would start to deteriorate as well. An ideal spot for displaying posters and various slogans bearing conflicting messages, it rapidly fell into disrepair through a combination of use and indifference. Dogs once more came along and urinated unconcernedly all over the gluey, ink-stained boards, which promptly disintegrated. Once they were broken off you had to turn your face away at the thought of what lay in the gaps. Sylvie Fabre, however, perfume bottle held aloft above the decaying piles, was fighting for her personal survival, braving the winds' erosion with all the strength of her two dimensions. Paul saw at times with some anxiety the blue being eroded little by little by the bare freestone pushing through and breaking a stitch in his mother's dress; but it was all a very gradual process.

One thing leads to another in the chain of events, invariably setting a seal on what has occurred and colouring what is to come next. Once the building permit is in your pocket, things move rapidly. Someone having no doubt sold his soul along with the building plot, a gaping hole opens up. So there was the hole, and in it piles of new earth of the kind you get in towns, no more sterile than most. Men in yellow hats dug steadily, systematically, with machines: two yellow bulldozers and a yellow crane. No flames came out of the broken fencing smouldering in one of the holes. Black spirals of smoke rose in the air. Pieces of red and white ribbon hung on rusty poles, delimiting the scene of operations. The foundations were laid, all the building materials delivered, and the superstructure erected; fresh planks of new wood covered in little lumps of cement lay everywhere. The storeys swallowed up Sylvie like the tide. Paul saw Fabre once on the site when the building was about to reach the height of his mother's waist. On another occasion, as it rose towards her breasts, the widower was talking to the foreman and unfolding a plan, correct to the nearest millimetre. Paul kept out of the way, out of reach of the irritating voice.

In place of the grassy area there would be a block of flats almost identical to the one that had replaced the old building, but with bow windows instead of little balconies.

Sometime later on, these two would be joined together, as though to guard the preserved Wagner building; they would cast their intersecting shadows protectively over its old zinc roof. But from the shoulders up, the site had become intolerable for her son, who had stopped going there as soon as her whole dress had been covered by the wall. Several weeks elapsed before he returned to the Quai de Valmy, and then it was only by chance. The building wasn't quite completed; they were slow to finish. Torn bags of cement lay around. The windows had been freshly puttied and still had blobs of white so that people would realize they were there. And it was more a sepulchre than an effigy of Sylvie. One approached it differently, with a step that was not so carefree.

You went through the entrance and there in the centre of a paved courtyard was a raised flowerbed, promising the return of the betrayed plant-life. Paul was just having a look at it when a woman coming along the pavement stopped and shouted, Fabre! Paul turned round, since it was, after all, his name, and again she shouted, Fabre! Fabre, I've got some milk! The shrill voice came from above, from a window somewhere up in the sky: You're joking, Jacqueline.

The unknown woman disappeared. Paul, come on up.

Things must have gone downhill during the time they had not seen one another, for there remained not one single large piece of furniture of those they had been able to afford with the insurance money after her death. Just a foam mattress pushed up against the right-hand wall, a small stove, and a trestle table on which lay some plans. Already specks of crumbs and bits of fluff pursued one another over the bare floor. But Fabre, apparently undeterred by his experience, was smartly dressed. He had cleaned the windows and through them you could see the bottom of the canal; there was no water in it because it was having its triennial emptying. Of murder weapons there was not much evidence. The only skeletons were the frames of old iron chairs and the corpses of mopeds; other than that just rims of wheels, split tyres, exhaust pipes, and handlebars. The amount of empty bottles seemed what one might expect, but the array of competing hypermarket trolleys was staggering. Everything was studded with stercoraceous snails wallowing in a sea of mud, being slowly siphoned out through the slimy tubes of huge pipes which every now and again emitted slurping noises.

Fabre had been first in the queue to rent, even before the painters had arrived. He displayed no interest in the show apartment. He could not be prevented from moving in straight away to the fourth floor of the Wagner side, into a studio flat right under the eyes of Sylvie, two pale lamps behind the wall on the right. According to his calculations, he was sleeping up against her smile, hanging from her lips as though in a hammock; he showed his son on the plans.

Fabre's voice going on about his special mission so grated on his son's nerves he felt like burying his head. Paul, in any case, left after twenty minutes.

He got some things together and went back on the Saturday evening. His father had been out shopping: another piece of foam, a few tools, supplies of yoghurt, crisps, and plenty of snacks. Under the naked light bulb neither of them spoke of what had happened to them in the last few years. They just talked about the need for a lamp-shade and then discussed the colour. Fabre was somewhat more inclined to talk than Paul. Before going to sleep he grumbled a little about the underfloor heating, as though thinking of his own comfort. Look how much sun we get! he also observed the next day.

It was true that the sun would flood the entire apart-ment, like a spotlight in a music-hall in a border zone. It was Sunday, and it was almost a matter for regret that there was so little noise coming from outside. As on all public holidays, meals would tend to run into one another, so they agreed on two o'clock; they would get down to it then. When it was as hot as this, Paul's father continued, you really felt like giving the whole damn thing up. They scarcely mentioned the complexity of the task, which would certainly call for not just patience and strength but the skills of an Egyptian archaeologist at the last. Fabre had sketched out details of all stages in the process on a separate schedule stapled to the plan. So, although not very hungry, they had their meal at about two. Their jaws ground out the minutes, they chewed according to the clock. Counting backwards like that you can decide at any point when it is to be zero hour. So you might as well get on with it straight away and start scraping; no need to change, because you are already in your baggy white working gear spattered with paint. Start scraping and layers of plaster hang in the sunshine, flaking onto foreheads and into forgotten cups of coffee. Scrape and scrape, then start to pant, to sweat, as it begins to get unbearably hot.

Iéna

Annie Saumont

At the battle of Jena[1] there is victory and defeat. And who would dare pretend it's only a game? Both sides have to count the cost. Let's behave as though there was no struggle, there were no losers. Jena. A battle leaves its scar on you. The real victim is always the one who is left for dead, regardless of which side they happen to be on.

Okay, I'll see you at Iéna, she says. I'll leave Montreuil at three. It doesn't take long. Twenty minutes. Unless, he says, some poor devil decides to chuck himself under the métro

---

[1] The battle of Jena, 14 October 1806, resulted in the victory of Napoleon over the Prussians. In common with other métro stations, the métro station Iéna commemorates an important battle.

after lunch and you're late, I'll be waiting for you as usual. I'm used to it. Oh for God's sake, shut up.

Torn to pieces, stabbed, smashed up, blown apart. Damned, crushed, mutilated, broken, eviscerated. Jena. The ones who couldn't escape conscription, flushed out of their holes; those who sold themselves for a song. The ones who only put on a uniform because they were after glory. Just for the hell of it. Out of bravado. Proud to serve a man who thought he was a god. Those who blamed Fate while the bullets were already passing through their bodies, when the bayonets were tearing their bellies apart and grapeshot ripping their balls off.

At Jena, those who will never know Johann Gottlieb Fichte[2] and his *Way to a Blessed Life*; those who will never again read—if they ever have, that is—Schiller or Goethe; those who are simply lying there or being carried off on makeshift stretchers to the surgeon with the ironmonger's saw, to the kindly but impotent hands of the women who are making linen dressings. At Jena, when the fog clears, the smell of gunpowder, the dull gold of the leaves, the blazing gold of the fires, those who believe in God and those who do not.

[2] Fichte, 1762–1814, the German philosopher, was a disciple of Kant. His '*Anweisung zum seligen Leben*' (*Way to a Blessed Life*) was published in the same year as the battle of Jena.

At Iéna, the twenty-second station of the Montreuil-Pont de Sèvres line, she gets out on to the platform, makes her way to the exit. Consults her watch.

She leans over, puts a coin in the tin the cripple is holding out. He is crouching, his crutches are leaning against the concrete wall where the graffiti writers have scrawled some enigmatic message.

At Jena the horses, hindquarters shuddering, fall back into the ditch. Normally when a horse is wounded, they put it down. But here there is no one left to administer the *coup de grâce*. At Jena the dead will have no place of burial. The Emperor has gone galloping by without condescending to work a miracle.

At Iéna, at the bend in the passage, she says, Sorry, when the tramps suddenly push against her, bawling and lurching. One has a bottle in his hand. She says, Oh sorry. He says, No worries. Another says, No problem. Both of them roar with laughter. The one brandishing the bottle, already the worse for wear, is yelling, Cheers, darling, it's good for you.

She declines his offer, climbs the steps.

Reaches the top. The corner of the two avenues. He is there. Eyes down, tone serious, I've got something to say to you . . . . We can't go on like this. Let's call it a day. Let's go and have a drink in the Goethe Institute. Classes start again soon. I'm teaching history this year. I'll show you the lecture theatre. You can always come and listen to me.

She says no. She doesn't need putting down. It's horses you put down. At least when there is one last horseman left. One soldier, defeated and exhausted, who hasn't thrown his gun away, crawling, dragging his lifeless legs along behind.

She leaves, crosses the Avenue d'Iéna, heedless of the cars. Hooters blast. Brakes screech. He watches her go. He sighs. Shrugs.

That's how it goes.

The Adventure

Cyrille Fleischman

He was no geographer, but he had come to the quasi-scientific conclusion that the centre of the world was directly above the métro Saint-Paul. Perhaps slightly to the right of the Rue Saint-Antoine, in the direction of the Rue Caron, where he lived. But certainly no farther away than that. Nearer the Bastille, it was another world entirely. Nearer Châtelet it was the jungle.

Jean Simpelberg was born in the Rue Caron. He lived in the Rue Caron; his parents, when they came over from Russia, had lived in the Rue Caron. Except during the war he had never left Paris. Not only had he not moved from his *quartier*, he had not even moved a hundred yards to the left or right, north or south of his block near the corner of the Rue Caron and the Place du Marché Sainte-Catherine.

He used to say to his wife:

'Tomorrow I'll go to the Samaritaine.'[1]

She would look at him:

'Last time you went to the bazaar at the Hôtel de Ville you were all done in. What is it you want to buy there?'

He'd answer: 'Screws, for mending the sideboard.'

'Screws? At this time of the year? At the Hôtel de Ville?'

Simpelberg, alarmed by the undertone of criticism, abandoned the idea of his trip. He would wait for the rainy season to end.

'Perhaps we can send the concierge's son,' he suggested tentatively. 'He can put on his raincoat and go and get them for me and come back this afternoon.'

'You're not going to put that child's health at risk just to mend the sideboard.'

And so Simpelberg would resign himself to staying on his own territory. However, he did permit himself a cunning ploy, which involved having to go slightly beyond his own frontiers. Without saying anything to his wife, he went as far as the ironmonger's in the Rue Saint-Antoine, nearly to the end of the street. For, since retiring from

---

[1] The famous department store in the Châtelet area, three métro stops from Saint-Paul.

his job as foreman in a workshop in the Rue de Turenne, Simpelberg would sometimes take a gamble on his domestic life.

He was not rich, but nor was he poor. Just a quiet pensioner who enjoyed the rhythm of the passing seasons in a little place whose station was the Saint-Paul métro.

He had children who would touch down from other, remote places like the fourteenth and fifteenth *arrondissements*, where, apparently, it was also possible to live. He had his doubts about that. He didn't resent his sons choosing to exile themselves, for he was convinced it was his daughters-in-law who had lured them away to these far-flung regions.

Every Friday evening the family met up in the Rue Caron to have dinner with the grandparents. There was the son who worked in a garage in the suburbs, his wife and the two grandsons; the son and the daughter-in-law who were both doctors in the fifteenth *arrondissement*. The daughter, as yet unmarried, but practically engaged to a student from the Cité Universitaire in the dim and distant area of the Parc Montsouris, brought him along too.

Simpelberg asked for news of the world outside and posed *the* question:

'When are you going to make up your minds to live a normal life and take a flat in the Rue Saint-Antoine or the Rue de Turenne, in our part of the world?'

The third generation of Simpelbergs smiled and they all said: 'We're fine where we are. We've got the car. Or the métro or bus, we are twenty minutes away. Don't worry about it.'

Ignoring them, he looked at his wife: 'Who's worrying? But is it normal to live quite so far away? Even just for the sake of the children: surely no park has better air than the Place des Vosges?'

The daughter-in-law from the fifteenth interposed: 'But you know very well that the air is polluted with all this traffic, and anyway these days there's nothing but rich people and concierges in the Place des Vosges.'

Simpelberg tapped on the table: 'The Place des Vosges polluted? Do I look polluted? Do I look rich? I spent the whole of my childhood playing in the Place des Vosges. I went to nursery school and primary school in the Place des Vosges!'

'Don't keep going on about yourself and your *quartier*. Paris is a big city. Just be thankful that we come every week. We could be living in the provinces, or abroad!'

He looked at his wife and said: 'They're being silly. Serve up the soup, it'll get cold.'

Mme Simpelberg put in: 'Young people want to live their own lives. It's a long way off, a very long way. But if they choose to ruin their health, what can we do about it?'

And she would utter a sigh as she plunged the ladle into the soup-tureen.

After they had drunk a tisane, and the children and grandchildren had gone back to their far-off homes, Simpelberg went to bed meditating upon the week's excitement.

He got into bed where his wife was already snoring gently, put out the bedside lamp, and after a few seconds fell asleep, on a good mattress, in cosiness and comfort.

And up there in Heaven guardian angels were watching over him.

The angels who were in charge of the men of action, the famous, the doers of great deeds, were consulting their monitors, and read: 'Ordinary men. No action required!'

Those who were in charge of the Simpelbergs of this life were busying themselves round machines whose message was: 'Extreme care! Men of Adventure. Must be protected.'

What Goes On in Saint-Germain

Anna Gavalda

Saint-Germain-des-Prés? I know what you are about to say: 'Darling, how banal! Sagan[1] did it a long time before you, and a whole lot better!'

I know.

But what do you expect? I'm not at all sure this would have happened to me on the Boulevard de Clichy. That's how it is. *C'est la vie.*

But keep your thoughts to yourself, and listen, for a little bird tells me you're going to enjoy this story.

You love sentimental tales. Titillating descriptions of

---

[1]   Françoise Sagan (born 1935) is the author of several bestselling novels, including *Bonjour Tristesse* (1954) and *Aimez-vous Brahms?* (1959).

evenings when something is about to happen; men who make you believe they are single and a bit lonely.

I know you adore all that. Quite right too. But no way can you read Harlequin romances when you are sitting in the Café Lipp or the Deux-Magots. You just can't, and that's all there is to it.

OK then, this morning I met someone on the Boulevard Saint-Germain.

I was just going back up the boulevard and he was coming down. We were on the side with the even numbers, the fashionable side.

I saw him coming a long way off. I don't know what it was about him, perhaps the rather nonchalant walk, or the way his coat swung casually open in front of him . . . . Well, anyway, I was twenty metres away and I already knew our paths were bound to cross.

It all went according to plan. When we drew level, I saw him glance in my direction. I flashed him a flirty smile, Cupid's arrow kind of stuff, but a bit more reserved.

He smiled at me too.

As I went on, I kept smiling, thinking of *La passante* by Baudelaire (you will have realized already from Sagan just now that I'm full of what are called literary allusions!!!). I walk more slowly, because I'm trying to remember . . . . *Longue, mince, en grand deuil* . . . . What comes next . . .? Um . . . *une femme passa, d'une main fastueuse, soulevant, balançant le feston et l'ourlet* . . . . And the last line . . . . *Ô toi que j'eusse aimée, ô toi qui le savais.*[2]

It gets me every time.

And meanwhile, how delightfully naïve! I feel the eyes of my Saint Sebastian—remember the arrow, don't you? I hope you're following the plot!?—still piercing my back. There is a delicious warmth on my shoulder-blades, but I'd die rather than turn round, it would spoil the poem.

I stopped on the edge of the pavement, watching the flow of traffic and waiting to cross opposite the Rue des Saints-Pères.

I should explain: no self-respecting Parisienne ever crosses the Boulevard Saint-Germain on the zebra crossing when the lights are red. She watches the flow of traffic and hurls herself forward, knowing she is taking her life in her hands.

Paule Ka's shop window is to die for. Exquisite.

I am about to hurl myself into the traffic when a voice makes me stop. I won't say it's a 'warm, manly voice' just to please you, because it wasn't. It was merely a voice.

'Excuse me . . .'

I turned round. Oh, who is it . . .? My handsome quarry of a moment ago.

---

[2] *Tall, slim, dressed all in black . . . a woman passed me, her jewelled hand lifting, swinging the festooned hem of her garlanded robe . . . . Oh you, whom I might have loved, oh you who knew that . . .*

I may as well tell you straight away, from that moment on Baudelaire didn't stand a chance.

'I was wondering if you would like to have supper with me this evening.'

In my head I am thinking, 'How romantic . . .' But I answer: 'You're a fast worker, aren't you?'

He retorted (and I promise you this is true): 'You're right, I am. But when I watched you disappearing I said to myself: how silly, I meet this woman in the street, I smile at her, she smiles at me, we brush against each other and now we are going to lose one another . . . . It's too stupid, no really it's frankly absurd.'

'. . .'

'Well, what do you think? Does what I am saying sound completely mad?'

'No, no, not at all.'

I was starting to feel a little queasy.

'Well then? What about it? Here, there, this evening, in a little while, at nine, at this exact spot?'

You need to get a grip, my dear. If you have to have dinner with all the men you smile at, you'll never be out of the wood . . .

'Give me one good reason to accept your invitation.'

'One good reason . . . . Heavens, that's difficult.'

I watch him, amused.

And then, without warning, he takes hold of my hand: 'I think I've found a good enough reason.'

He puts my hand on his unshaven cheek. 'One good reason. Here it is: say yes, so I'll have to shave. Honestly, I think I look much better when I've had a shave.'

And he lets go of my arm.

'Yes,' I say.

'Excellent! Let's cross together, shall we? I shouldn't want to lose you now.'

This time I'm the one watching him go off in the opposite direction. He must be rubbing his cheeks like a man who's just clinched a deal . . . .

I bet he's well pleased with himself. And so he should be.

A bit nervous by the end of the afternoon, I have to admit.

The trick has backfired on me and I can't decide what to wear. The patent leather might be a good idea.

A bit nervous, like a debutante who knows her hairdo is a disaster.

A bit nervous, as though I'm about to embark on a love affair.

I work, answer the phone, send faxes, finish a layout for the designer. (Just a sec, well yes, of course . . . a pretty girl with a bit of go in her who sends faxes in the area of Saint-Germain-des-Prés is obviously going to be in publishing.)

My fingertips are frozen and I have to ask people to repeat everything they say to me.

Deep breath, girl, deep breath . . .

Dusk, and the boulevard has gone quiet; the cars have got their sidelights on.

The café tables are being taken in, people are waiting for each other on the steps of the church, others are queueing at the Beauregard to see the latest Woody Allen.

I can't in all decency arrive first. No. And better to arrive a little late. It would be a good idea to make him hang around a bit.

I'll go and have a little pick-me-up to put some warmth in my fingers.

Not in the Deux-Magots, that's slightly vulgar at night; nothing but fat American women trying to recapture the spirit of Simone de Beauvoir.[3] I go to the Rue Saint-Benoit. Le Chiquito will do fine.

I push open the door, and I am hit by: the smell of beer mingling with stale tobacco, the pinging of the pinball machine, the priestess of the bar with her dyed hair and nylon blouse, through which you can see her massive underwired bra, the evening race at Vincennes going on in the background, a few builders in their stained overalls putting off the moment when they have to go back to their wives or their empty rooms, and old habitués with yellow fingers getting on everyone's nerves with the rent they used to pay in 1948. The good life.

<hr>

[3] Feminist writer and philosopher, Simone de Beauvoir (1908–86) who, with her companion Jean-Paul Sartre, frequented this famous café in the 1940s.

Now and then the men drinking at the counter turn their heads, sniggering like schoolboys. My legs, which are very long, are protruding into the space between the tables. The gap is quite narrow and my skirt is very short. I see their hunched backs shaking in fits and starts.

I smoke a cigarette, blowing the smoke a long way out. I look vaguely into the distance. I now know that it is Beautiful Day who has won on the home straight at ten to one.

I remember that I've got *Kennedy and Me*[4] in my bag and wonder if I shouldn't do better to stay where I am.

A little dish of lentils and half a jug of rosé . . . . Just the job . . .

But I pull myself together. You're there looking over my shoulder, hoping for love (or less? or more? or not exactly that?) like me, and I'm not going to stand you up with the barlady in the Chiquito. That would be a bit steep.

I come out with roses in my cheeks; the cold stings my legs.

There he is at the corner of the Rue des Saints-Pères, waiting for me, he sees me, and comes to meet me.

'I was scared. I thought you wouldn't come. I saw my reflection in the shop window, I admired my smooth cheeks and I was scared.'

---

[4] *Kennedy et moi* (1996), a novel by Jean-Paul Dubois.

'I'm sorry. I was waiting for the result of the evening race at Vincennes and didn't notice the time.'

'Who won?'

'Do you bet?'

'No.'

'Beautiful Day won.'

'Well of course, I should have guessed,' he smiled, taking my arm.

We walked in silence to the Rue Saint-Jacques. From time to time he threw a covert glance at me, studying my profile, but I know that at that moment he was wondering if I was wearing tights or stockings.

Patience, my dear, patience . . .

'I'm going to take you to one of my favourite places.'

I know the kind of place, with relaxed but obsequious waiters who smile at him with a conspiratorial air: 'Bonssouar monsieur . . . . (So this is the latest one . . . . Well I liked the dark-haired girl from last time better . . .) The little table at the back as usual, monsieur . . .?' Bowing and scraping. '(Where on earth does he dig up all these women?) May I take your coats? Thank you.'

He gets them from off the street, you idiot.

But no. It wasn't like that.

He let me go in first, holding the door of a little wine bar open for me, and a surly waiter simply asked if we wanted smoking or non-smoking. That was all.

He hung our things on the hanger, and when he caught

a glimpse of my charmingly low neckline in one idle split second, I knew he was not sorry about the little cut he had made on his chin when he was shaving a short while before and his hands had let him down.

We drank extraordinary wine in great big wine glasses. We ate rather fine food, carefully chosen not to spoil the bouquet of our nectar.

One bottle of Côte-de-Nuits, Gevray-Chambertin 1986. Sweet and smooth as velvet.

The man sitting opposite me is screwing up his eyes as he drinks.

I have got to know him better.

He is wearing a grey polo-neck made of cashmere. An old polo-neck. At the elbows he's got patches, and there's a little tear near the right cuff. Perhaps he had it for his twentieth birthday. His mum, worried by his disappointed expression, saying: 'You'll be glad of it, you know . . .' and giving him a kiss and a hug.

A very understated jacket which looks just like what it is, a tweed jacket; but as I am me, and have eyes like a lynx, I can tell it's made to measure. At Old England, the labels are wider when the products come straight from the workshop in the Rue des Capucines, and I saw the label when he leaned down to pick up his serviette.

His serviette that he dropped on purpose so that he could set his mind at rest on the subject of the stockings, I imagine.

He talks about a lot of things but never about himself. He always has a problem picking up the thread of his story when I allow my hand to rest on my neck. He says: 'And what about you?' But I don't talk about myself either.

While we are waiting for dessert, my foot touches his ankle.

He puts his hand on mine and then pulls it back suddenly because the sorbets arrive.

He says something but no sound comes out and I hear nothing.

We are both excited.

Oh horror! His mobile has just gone off.

All eyes in the restaurant are focused upon him. He swiftly switches it off. No doubt he has just ruined a great deal of fine wine. It goes down badly, down irritated throats. People are choking, their fingers clenched over the handles of their knives or the folds in their starched napkins.

Those damned machines, there's always one, whenever, it doesn't matter where you are.

What a jerk.

He's embarrassed. Suddenly he feels a bit hot under his mum's cashmere jumper.

He nods towards various people as if to signal his confusion. He looks at me and his shoulders slump a little.

'I'm awfully sorry . . .' He is still smiling at me, but perhaps not so aggressively.

I say: 'Don't worry. We're not in the cinema. One day I shall kill somebody. A man or woman who answers the phone while the film is on. And when you read it in the local paper, you'll know it's me . . . .'

'I'll know it's you.'

'Do you read the local paper?'

'No, but I'll start if I think you might be in them.'

The sorbets were, what shall I say?, delicious.

My Prince Charming, by now restored, came to sit next to me while we had our coffee.

So close now, he knows for sure. I am definitely wearing stockings. He has felt the little hook at the top of my thighs.

I know at that moment he has forgotten everything else.

He lifts my hair and kisses the nape of my neck, the small hollow at the back.

He whispers in my ear that he adores the Boulevard Saint-Germain, that he adores burgundy and blackcurrant sorbet.

I kiss the little cut on his chin. I apply myself to it. For some time, I have had in mind to do just that.

The coffees, the bill, the tip, our coats, just so many details now. Unimportant things holding us back.

Our hearts are thumping.

He hands me my black coat and then . . .

I admire his technique, with his hat pulled down, it's oh-so-discreet, scarcely visible, really well calculated and awfully well carried out: as he places my coat on my naked shoulders, inviting and soft as silk, he manages to find the necessary split-second and the perfect angle, leaning towards the inside pocket of his jacket, to check the messages on his mobile.

I come to my senses. All at once.

Traitor.

Wretch.

What have you done, you miserable creature!?

What were you busy doing when my shoulders were so round and warm and your hand so near!?

What did you have to do that seemed more important than my breasts inviting your gaze?

What were you so bothered about when I was waiting for your breath upon my back?

Could you not have fiddled with your wretched machine after—and only after—you'd made love to me?

I button my coat right up to the top.

Out in the street I am cold, tired, and I feel sick.

I ask him if he'll come with me to the first taxi rank.

He is horrified.

Call the emergency services, old chap, you've got what you need.

But no, he remains cool.

As if there were nothing in the least wrong. Just, I'm seeing a good friend into a taxi, I'm rubbing her arms to warm her up, and making conversation about Paris at night.

A touch of class from start to finish, I have to admit.

Before I get into a black Mercedes taxi with a Val-de-Marne number plate, he says: 'But . . . we'll see each other again, won't we? I don't even know where you live . . . . Leave me something, an address, a phone number . . . .'

He tears a strip of paper from his diary and scribbles down the numbers.

'Here. The first number's my home, the second's my mobile, and you can get me on that whenever . . .'

I was already aware of that.

'Don't hesitate, mind, any time, OK? I'll wait for you to call.'

I ask the driver to drop me at the top of the boulevard because I need to walk.

I aim a few kicks at non-existent tin cans.

I hate mobile phones, I hate Sagan, I hate Baudelaire and all such charlatans.

I hate my pride.

Manuscript Found at Saint-Germain-des-Prés

Frédéric Beigbeder

I'm sitting upstairs in the Flore[1] for the last time. I'm enjoying my last glass of Coca-Cola Heavy. Soon it will all be over. They are on their way. At the bottom of the Boulevard Saint-Germain, you can already hear their shouts, the deathly war-cries, the deafening noise of the home-made hand-grenades exploding in the fashion boutiques, at John Lobb, and in the Crédit Lyonnais offices in the Rue du Bac. ... They are not far off.

I'm writing these few words in a desperate hurry. It's not a last testament because I have nothing to leave. Everything I have ever known is going to vanish. No one will be

---

[1] The Flore was a café frequented by Jean-Paul Sartre in the 1940s.

surprised at our demise. In centuries to come history books will list the causes of what has happened: the disappointment of the Mitterrand years, then the Chirac years, the breakdown of society, as it was called . . . . But I find it very odd that I have to die on 10 May.[2] A strange anniversary. I hope they won't be too hard on me, that it will be over quickly. That I shall be despatched swiftly.

We must admit we have richly deserved it. It all started when the *mairie* of the sixth *arrondissement* decided to expel the SDF[3] from the Rue du Dragon. What a ludicrous idea it was to allow them to move in in the first place: the worm was in the apple. For a whole year they were in a position to observe our opulent lifestyle, our shops full of luxurious clothes, our restaurants that make you want to throw up, our clubs they are excluded from, our sports cars parked all over the road, our fucked-up models and show-biz personalities, all the heap of rubbish we have been displaying quite shamelessly outside the DAL.[4] How could we have suspected that this building was their Trojan Horse?

---

[2] May has often been the month in which revolutions or political struggles have taken place, for example the bloody defeat of the Commune in 1871 and the students' revolt in May 1968. On 10 May 1968, there was a particularly violent night of rioting in the Latin Quarter, with police assaults, cars burned, and hundreds of people hospitalized.

[3] Sans Domicile Fixe, literally 'of no fixed abode'.

[4] The Droit au Logement (DAL), or Right to Lodging, was created in 1990 by Paris families who had been evicted from houses where they had been squatting.

Jacques Chirac was elected in May 1995 through a curious misunderstanding. I smile as I write this euphemism, for, outside, I can hear the throbbing of the last helicopter of our private security militia. It's just as well the militia's there. If we had to rely on the police alone for our protection . . .

Perhaps I shall have a short breathing space to finish this piece. Forgive me if I mix everything up. I don't think I shall have time to read through what I've written.

The eviction from the Rue du Dragon most certainly went very badly. The cyber-police must have fought in non-virtual combat every inch of the way. There were no end of dead in both camps. It was war as it was actually happening, on Telefrance+, the class struggle all over again, rich against poor (best television ratings of the year).

After that, the Madelin government told us we had to look out for ourselves. And that's when the idea of the Wall of Saint-Germain-des-Prés came into being. At the beginning of the year they began to build a rampart three metres high all round the *quartier*. It contained the Rue Jacob, the former First Minister's residence, the Rue des Saints-Pères, the Rue du Four, and the Rue de Seine, protecting our village against possible invaders. A magnificent architectural achievement, designed by Philippe Starck,[5] with thermal cameras and laser-miradors. A door-to-door collection

---

[5]   Successful Parisian designer of everything from pasta to palaces.

financed its construction, just as it did for the purchase of the remote-control helicopters for the Saint-Germain militia.

Those were good times. We could again go out in complete safety in the *quartier*. The Germanopratins[6] had smiles on their faces once more. Celebrations were organized everywhere and all the apartments were open day and night. You could leave the keys in the ignition of your Ferrari and not worry. At night only the lights shining down from the surveillance helicopters pierced the darkness above the Brasserie Lipp.

Meanwhile the rest of the country outside this perimeter was, of course, already on fire and running with blood.

The noise is getting nearer. My hand is trembling with fear, for I am a coward. I don't want to die, for Christ's sake. I already know I'll be down grovelling to them, like a piece of shit. I wanted to hang on to my money and leave those on the outside to manage as best they could. But, hell, I was just like everyone else, I didn't think the situation would deteriorate so fast!

Of course, the day they disembowelled Bernard-Henri Lévy[7] and Arielle Dombasle[8]—even though they had gone

---

[6] The inhabitants of Saint-Germain.

[7] Philosopher, writer, author of, among others, 'La Barbarie à visage humain' ('Barbarity with a Human Face').

[8] Film star, married to Bernard-Henri Lévy and mainly known for her role in Rohmer's 'Pauline à la Plage' ('Pauline at the Beach').

out quietly to meet them and begin a dialogue—I should have realized our turn would come. But, like everyone else, I thought it must be only an isolated incident . . . . And then there was the collective rape of Claudia Schiffer[9] (best ratings of Telefrance+ this year) and I well remember that we all hoped the gang-bang might calm them down a bit.

When they burned Matthieu Kassovitz,[10] our eyes were finally opened, but it was too late . . . The rest is history: the terrorist attack at Castel's, the bomb at Grasset's, the terrible hanging of Philippe Sollers[11] by the feet from the belltower of Saint-Germain-des-Prés . . . .

I've sent my last two bodyguards out to reconnoitre the boulevard. What can they be doing? They should have got the 3D video to me on my Microsoft-Swatch ten minutes ago.

We reap what we have sown. Ah, yes, the fall of communism, we celebrated that all right! That time capitalism won. How blind we were! All the questions raised by Karl Marx were still raised, but a hundred thousand times more violently. We thought it quite normal that a tiny minority of privileged people should control an immense majority of the destitute. Our gigantic apartments seemed perfectly all

---

[9] Top model and sex symbol.

[10] Controversial film director of films such as 'La Haine' ('Hatred').

[11] Novelist and critic, founder of the review *Tel Quel* and *L'Infini* at Gallimard.

right to us. We were blind to the unbearable obscenity of our lives.

I have just seen the head of one of my bodyguards through the window, on the end of a pike, his eyes bulging. They have entered the Flore. Come back, Sartre, they've all gone mad! I scribble you this farewell, locked in the lavatory. There is a noise of steps on the stairs. Here they are. They are banging at the door.

I somehow doubt if I shall manage to make friends with them.

ALLÉE
Jacques GARNERIN
PREMIER PARACHUTISTE
1769 - 1823

Blind Experiment

Hugo Marsan

He never spends much time in the main avenue of the Parc Monceau, where there is a constant stream of people taking a short cut to work. He likes shade and privacy. You must enter via the Boulevard Malesherbes if you want to see him. After passing through one of the three great heavy wrought-iron gates, stippled with gold, you cross the Avenue Vélasquez to the second gate which is similar, a few yards further on, and turn left into the *allée* A-J Garnerin. André-Jacques Garnerin—he has looked it up in the encyclo-pedia—is the parachutist who, in 1797, dared to throw himself out of the sky.

There he is, sitting on one of the green benches ranged at intervals along the path. At recreation columns of children break up and disperse. The boys scatter over the grass. The girls watch them. Slim young women supervise. The windows of a private school open out on to the park. You can see pictures of Father Christmas and cut-out snow scenes stuck on to the windows.

He sits on the same bench at three o'clock every afternoon. The apple-eating secretaries, lifting their faces to the pale sun, and the impatient businessmen clutching their mobile phones have already left. He has walked from the Rue Pelletier in the ninth *arrondissement*, where he has rented an attic room ever since he was a student.

On Saturdays and Sundays you never see the young man in the Parc Monceau. The two women don't ever go for a walk on those days; he has checked. He misses them, but is glad they are not there. The weekend crowds would get in the way of his waiting. The Companion, as he calls her, after a film he especially liked, must be the elderly lady's oldest daughter, and for those two days she entrusts her mother to some member of the family. The Companion is no longer young, but her body is slim and supple. Her face—or what he divined of it the very first time he saw her—is beautiful, as a lake is beautiful, since she has long since stopped caring whether men look at her or not.

On Saturdays and Sundays he really misses her, but tells himself she needs to rest and have some respite. To enjoy her private life, he thinks, although he is convinced that she no longer has a private life, alone with her memories of a passionate love affair. Private life . . . But he takes comfort from these two words which hold the promise of sweet, solemn hours together in the quiet of a shady apartment, at the back of a courtyard full of trees, in this well-heeled *quartier* where the façades suggest a discreet voluptuousness, a luxurious melancholy. On Sundays she lies on a brown velvet couch and reads. She puts on her spectacles which hang on a gold chain round her neck. Bookshelves line the walls. The night before, she has been to a concert with a woman friend who is keen on music. Certainly, they enjoy the piano—Mozart, Chopin, Satie. The friend also likes being on her own and they soon tire of each other's company. When they leave the concert hall they go their own ways. They prefer their ghosts, a melancholy that has become familiar to them, beyond forgetting, beyond suffering. On Monday the leisurely walks begin again. He revels in their affection. A girl who loves her mother.

They were walking along the *allée* where the young man comes to wait for them each weekday. He wants to catch them off guard in that moment he has so eagerly anticipated, when she bends over the old lady and anxiously, tenderly, scrutinizes her face, to discern the marks of her own old age, searching nevertheless for a glimmer of hope in the depths of those dim eyes. She had been to the hairdresser. The same cut, heavy hair thrown back, but shorter, more lustrous. Her fight against time does not go beyond the rituals of daily care. The beauty parlour perhaps once a month. But no surgical cosmetics, oh no! The young man on the bench smiles: she would never do that!

The last days of autumn in the Parc Monceau are flame-coloured, quiet, red and gold, just like in a novel by Louis Bromfield which she must have read in her youth. Everything tidy, the green benches in the shade newly cleaned, the clothes of the two women comfortable and discreet, the statues smooth, the light warm and intense, occasionally shattered by the echo of a child's shout. He bursts out laughing. No, nothing artificial, she is beautiful enough as it is. I'll be there to love her, to look after her. We shall be the same age for ever.

There are not many young people in the Parc Monceau. A few au pairs pushing prams, dreamy blondes, serious-looking black people walking straight and tall. Old men, sad old men proceeding slowly, painstakingly. The young man is safe. He never spares a thought for the hospital where, two mornings a week, he undergoes the tests, X-rays, scans, and blood samples which are all part of the Procedure. He does not make a fuss about taking the medication—the placebos, he reassures Juliette, though he does not believe it—that they are trying out on him. It was a respectable, discreet way of earning a bit of money. A totally passive way, Juliette shrieked at him. Passive and irresponsible. You don't even know what they are making you swallow. It will be the death of you; they can't tell themselves what the consequences will be in the long term, in one year, or ten, or even later, and one day when you can't even remember that you ever were a guinea-pig, you'll fall ill. He had tried to reason with her. Had he not answered the advert in an important daily? It was very serious, medical, scientific. They wore white uniforms. They had light, reassuring voices. They took every precaution. He had signed an agreement. I'm in the blind experiment group, he explained to Juliette, as though the expression were the ultimate guarantee. She had shut him up. Blind, you can say that again! She shrugged. Well, you are a grown man . . . and I suppose you think you're immune. Juliette was talkative, dynamic, impossibly young. She believed in living, set up projects, planned journals, invented diets, and did gymnastics three times a week. Juliette, the eternal optimist, was always rushing around. She tired and often scared him. He never breathed a word about the Parc Monceau to her.

The Companion holds on firmly to the old lady's arm. She never increases the pace. Their walk unfolds, like a very old film that has been slowed down. Their clothes look the same, vary only minutely according to the day and the weather. Tones of beige; those subtle shades his own mother had explained to him when he lived in cosy intimacy with her: ecru, eggshell, ivory, bisque, sand, honey . . . the non-colours. That's how rich people conceal themselves from the poor and recognize one another, she told him.

The old lady stops, pointing at a bird that has come to perch on the ground in front of them. A blackbird, she says, a blackbird, in her delighted little girl's voice. She turns round and her face lights up: a blackbird . . . Yes, it's a black-bird, says the Companion encouragingly, that's right. Gently she takes her hand and slowly strokes it, from finger-tips to wrist, lightly touching the large purple veins beneath the translucent skin. Do you remember there were birds in the country, in the garden? Do you remember the house, the birds in the trees, their singing? Tell me about the house and the birds. But the old lady is already rooted to the spot, teetering in the middle of the path. The bird flies away. She utters a little cry of disappointment.

The young man's eyes have feasted on the long, elegant fingers clasping the wrinkled and deformed hand. That soothing hand, he wants it for himself. Just your hand on mine and your grave face bent over me.

That unbearable image again flashes into his mind. The young man in the Parc Monceau sees his mother's hand, talon-like, hanging on to his arm. He cannot pull those claws away. His mother's mouth is wide and drawing in, with a terrifying sucking sound, the small amount of air that, in spite of all her efforts, cannot bring her back to life. You can't abandon her like that. He insults the nurse. Calm down, Monsieur, the morphine is not working any longer.

But she does not want to die! Please, young man, a little respect, the nurse reprimands him. Soon there is a rattle. He can hardly recognize his mother in this woman, reduced to her last breath. It's over, the senior doctor had declared. His mother's hand was soldered to his arm and her haggard eyes fixed upon him. Her eyes fixed to the window of her eternal prison, as he lamented to Juliette when she came to join him. But Juliette had no time for misfortune or grieving.

The woman of the Parc Monceau had gone round a second time. When they passed him again—the old lady had once more relapsed into silence—he followed them. They went out by the Avenue Van Dyck, on the east side. They disappeared behind the door of 48, Rue Murillo. From the pavement opposite he spied the shadows behind the windows. What revelation was he expecting? The pink brick façade gave nothing away. He was about to leave when the Companion came out again. She walked briskly to a black Austin and opened the door. The car, with a 92 number plate, pulled away. Was she going back to her children, a husband, another life?

During the Christmas holidays his appointments at the hospital stopped. He took the train for Poitiers where Juliette taught mathematics. She had rented a house ten kilometres from the school. She loved the country, the fields, the woods, the outdoor life. On Boxing Day the storm broke. Trees fell all around them. One of the chimneys came down, bringing down the television aerial with it. They listened to the radio, and Juliette of course congratulated herself on having spare batteries. The trains stopped. Poitiers station was flooded. They were cut off, without electricity, muffled up in pullovers and blankets, by candlelight, next to the flame from the cooker. Juliette took great delight in displaying her organizational skills. These events gave her the opportunity to make use of all the things he had made fun of: the stores of provisions, stockpiled wood, and candlesticks placed all around the huge house. I told you so, she said, carrying in logs. He retorted that her manias and her physical courage were simply masks for fighting off melancholy. When she became angry and accused him of being fatalistic, he informed her she was an active depressive. Being shut up together like this was a disaster. His return was delayed and he could not talk to Juliette about the one thing that tormented him: would he ever see the two women in the Parc Monceau again?

Monday 3 January[1] and the gates were locked. From the confines of Juliette's house, he had not for one moment supposed that the storm that had raged in the Paris area could possibly have damaged the park. The jogging enthusiasts,

---

[1] 100-m.p.h. storms in Paris and in other regions just after Christmas, 1999, devastated large areas of forest and parkland.

drawn there by habit, were running round the outside, as near as they could to the old track. Curious onlookers stopped in front of the railings and sighed when they saw the decimated trees, their trunks laid out in lines across the paths. Like the joggers, he went round the outside of the park, first along the wide pavement on the Boulevard de Courcelles, then around the buildings that gave directly on to the park, where he found the roads paralysed and silent.

He came back each day, hoping it would reopen. And every day at three he waited for the door of 48 Rue Murillo to disclose the two women, or for the black Austin to come and pull up outside. For two months he watched in vain. He kept up his visits to the hospital. He submitted to the injections without flinching, swallowed the pills, gave careful answers to the senior doctor's questions. He liked the quiet atmosphere of the laboratory, the anodyne, polite conversation, which disguised what was going on on the quiet. Professor M. thanked him for his excellent cooperation.

He no longer went to Poitiers. Juliette came to Paris two weekends. They slept in the attic room, on a narrow mattress. They tried unconvincingly to revive their desire. Juliette blamed him: if he really loved her he would change his ways. In the end he said he didn't want to change his ways. So she concluded that he did not love her. The storm has spoiled everything, she told him; even what I thought was our love. He did not answer her. She called him immature, mad, criminal. Other women before her had used the same words. She blamed herself for not detecting in him before now the coward he had always been. Love is blind, she repeated, like your bloody medical Procedure. He did not admit that the only woman he could love was the woman from the Parc Monceau. He spared Juliette and let her be the one to break it off.

On Monday 20 March the park reopened. You will find the date underlined in the young man's diary. The trees that had survived were starting to blossom. He has sat down on the green bench and there, at the first turning in the *allée* bearing the name of the first parachutist, are two distinct silhouettes becoming larger, drawing nearer; he rises from the bench. He is not dreaming, the two women are stopping and the Companion is smiling at him. That is when he notices that the old lady is not the same as the December one. He does not ask why. All in good time.

He goes towards them. The old lady fixes her vacant eyes upon him. The voice of the Companion is clear and gentle, like those of some of the nurses in the hospital where he has gone that very morning to be told that his Procedure is coming to an end. They would contact him, probably in six months' time. But if you are worried about anything, anything at all, don't hesitate to get in touch, the specialist said. Here you are, I can always be reached on this number.

Would you like to walk with us? the Companion enquires.

I should love to, he stammers.

Take my arm . . . Careful, she adds with a smile, you are not on your own, slow down a bit, there's no hurry, we have plenty of time.

Yes, yes, plenty of time.

The old lady, smaller, and more decrepit than the other one, often stops and sighs. Children brush past them, their joy infectious. The gardeners are planting young trees. The sky is blue.

The other person, do you remember, the one from before Christmas? . . . You realize she died? She died during the storm. We had just got back from our walk. She fell. A small tree struck down.

I'm so sorry your mother died . . . .

It wasn't my mother! She laughs: you thought it was my mother?

Yes, I thought so, you seemed to be so close . . . .

I am always close to them.

He waits for them each afternoon and the three of them go slowly round the park. They accompany the old lady to the Rue de Lisbonne. He waits patiently outside the block of flats. She apologizes for keeping him waiting, thanks him, and stoops as she inserts her tall figure into the black Austin. See you tomorrow, she says. She waves her lovely hand. He crosses back through the park. Blackbirds fly off from under his feet. A red and green ball hits him on the leg.

He sends it back to the children with a well-aimed kick. He is happy.

You will no doubt be surprised to find him again in the summer, walking along on the Companion's arm. The second old lady is dead. She has not taken on another client. I know you do not care for the term 'client'. Should I say 'patient'? The young man does not care what you call them. She is his, all his. That is what she has suggested to him, smilingly. Do you want me to devote myself totally to you? He murmurs: But . . . the money? I don't have enough money to pay you . . . not enough . . . She strokes the young man's hand with an expert hand. Don't worry about the money. Money isn't everything. She places her lips upon the young man's cheeks. Scents of childhood invade the Parc Monceau. Into his head comes the image of the house again, a former station where his grandmother lived, and the straight path lined with lime trees leading to the cemetery.

There they are, then, the pair of them, advancing along the circular walk. She has put her arm under his. She is holding him up. If you are ever so slightly observant you will notice that he walks with difficulty, that his hand sometimes shakes when he points to a blackbird landing on the grass. You will also note that his hair, which was so black last year, is streaked with white. Yet his eyes still shine with happiness. Sometimes they sit down, the air is so warm. Moreover they have put back the time for their meeting.

They wait for the coolness of the evening, and leave each other a few minutes before the gardens close.

She knows that it never happens in the park, which is a place where time stands still. But she is afraid. The orders she carries out are never very precise. They have concealed certain details of the arrangement from her. She no longer communicates with them since they found out she is not charging. The young man gets more and more tired and takes the bus when he goes to meet her. In autumn you will see them still beneath the crimson leaves. She is still beautiful, perhaps more serious, and sometimes despairing, though she may smile as she bends over him.

Winter is coming. The children have stuck their Christmas drawings on the windows of the school. The branches are losing their leaves. The young man and his Companion have disappeared some time ago. You realize this, and are sad. Then to your great relief, you see them coming back, pressed one against the other. Your joy is shortlived. He has changed so much. And you can tell too that, after him, for her there will be no more visits to the Parc Monceau. He will be her last client.

Feeding the Hungry

Vincent Ravalec

He first came to Paris in the seventies, just after he had finished his police training. He was on duty at the Cité headquarters to begin with, and then patrolled the asphalt outside the embassies in the seventeenth *arrondissement*, before landing the kind of work he really wanted, riding his moped all over the capital.

Whenever he had three days' leave he went up north to his parents' place. They lived just this side of the Belgian border but, as the years went by, it became more and more difficult to go back after the weekend.

What he simply could not stand was people complaining the whole time. Everybody moaning and groaning, from the driver you pulled over for a faulty headlight to the cross-dresser at the Porte de Clignancourt. It was like an endless scream, it went on and on, it echoed in his eardrums for ages afterwards. Please, Monsieur, I beg you, please listen to me, Officer. I swear I'm insured. Those marks on my arm, that's not drugs, it's the treatment I'm having. I didn't nick the car radio, it was lying around on a window-sill, and anyway I've got my ID; now would I have my ID if I stole car radios? I'm having a bad time at the moment, Monsieur, a hell of a time, I can't see any way out of it, you wouldn't want my kids to die, would you? The litany of excuses went on and on.

And he would weigh everything up: yes, no, your papers aren't in order; and although he tried to remain fair and impartial, he invariably blew it in the end. Damn and blast your moaning, if I have to listen to any more of this crap I shall lose it. If you haven't got your documents for the car that's tough; it's not my fault and the car radio is stolen goods, it's coded, you shouldn't have been so daft as to buy it at Barbès. STOP MOANING!

Stop moaning.

His folks were not well off, far from it, but it wasn't the same for them. They had nothing in common with these pathetic no-hopers that he came across every day. And, most important of all, they were out in the country, where there was a bit of peace and quiet. There wasn't this noise, the mad rush all the time: stop, go, neon signs and flashing lights. Even people who didn't have a lot of money managed pretty well there, just about OK, and could sleep at night without being disturbed by the din of cars or young people racketing around.

He had a real thing about the young. Perhaps it was because he was getting on a bit or that people really were different now from how they used to be, but he was shocked at their fuck off, bugger off, you queer, you bastard, you mother-fucker; at twelve they were smoking joints and sometimes even pushing dope, all of them with their stolen mountain bikes, why the hell should I work my arse off?, everyone's on the dole, they tell you that all the time on the telly, there's no reason why it should change. You think I'm going to study, what's the point, I can earn more in two days than my old man gets in a month?

And the graffiti all over the place drove him round the bend, it made him feel like screaming out loud. The blocks of flats, cleaned and whitened, not a spot on them, any amount of money spent on restoring a bit of respectability to deprived areas and all those wretched kids going along behind squirting their cans of spray-paint—look at me, everybody, here I am, I've made a big mess, I'm the greatest, I'm the best.

Dogs in the gutter behaved better than that.

Some nights he lay awake, thinking. In the Dark Ages people died of hunger, in filth and poverty, today most people owned a telly, so what exactly was going wrong?

In the beginning he had believed in his vocation. Police-men are vital. We are the guarantors of democracy. Take away the uniform and the next thing you know it'll be gun law on the streets of Paris. Some degree of order is the basis for everything. The beginnings of organization and justice. On the fringes of society there were the ones who had to be kept from harming others, the rotten apples you take out of the fruit-dish, exactly like that. It was of course the job security and attractive salary which had drawn him to a career in the force, but he did have ideals nonetheless. Being a cop wasn't just any old job, even if he was in uniform and on a moped.

All of this was churning over and over in his mind, but truth to tell, he had had enough. Enough of the town, and of work, enough of sharing a locker, and of the foul smell of stale tobacco at the police station. He'd had it up to here with their please, Officer, please Chief, just one cigarette and can you do anything about my parking-ticket, I'm only on the dole and my son's got Aids. OH FUCK OFF THE LOT OF YOU!

Soon he would be able to enjoy his retirement and a quiet life. He was going to do up his parents' house and live quietly at home, doing a bit of DIY, possibly buying a little café or grocery business, he hadn't quite decided, and now he was counting the days. Another three years. Two years and eight months. Just two years and he would be shot of it. And it would not exactly be the delights of the Eiffel Tower he would remember.

About a year before the nightmare ended, he won on the lottery.

An unheard-of sum, a staggering amount.

Thirty-eight million francs.

He had done it for years but without ever expecting anything very much, and to say that winning was one of his obsessions was a long way from the truth. He liked money, he needed it like everyone else, but that was all. Not to the extent of dreaming about it at night.

Thirty-eight million francs.

It was such a huge sum you couldn't imagine how much, nor how it had happened, or anything.

At the office where they paid out you could choose to remain anonymous or have the publicity. Everyone advised him to go public—the idea of a policeman on a moped winning the lottery was perfect—but he opted for anonymity. He still had a few more months to do in the service, he might as well finish the job properly. The lottery and chance were all very well, but there was no point in working your backside off till then just to have your retirement points ruined in thirty seconds.

His life would have become unliveable if he had told

everybody; he would have had to resign and there was no question of that.

On 28 January his colleagues gave him a bit of a send-off in the mess. Lucky beggar, now you can do what you want, it'll be a great life. And that was exactly what he was thinking: thirty-eight million and off back home to retire.

At eleven a taxi was waiting for him as he left the police station.

He had already begun to enjoy himself on the quiet. Whenever he pulled a vehicle over he meticulously examined all the things wrong with it. You've got a broken bumper and it's a danger to pedestrians, Monsieur, and your disc isn't displayed, and suddenly the driver had to pay the full whack, and people were just about in tears, a 2,400-franc fine, and he would book him, inwardly pleased as punch: he had put 500-franc notes between the papers, far in excess of the fine. Ah, you gang of morons, you can't complain now that fate isn't kind to you.

He could just imagine the guy's ashamed, hang-dog expression as he sat there miserably in his car examining the dreadful wad of papers: 2,400 francs, how on earth am I going to be able to pay that—oh, am I dreaming or what? It looks as though there's some cash in there too.

He thrilled with happiness at the thought. You bet there's some cash in there, mate. I've done my duty and yet you will remember me with pleasure.

With very great pleasure.

The taxi-driver came from the Antilles. He had ordered him in the afternoon and booked him for the whole night. As soon as he got in he warned the man: I'll pay whatever you ask, but I don't want you to pass any comments. Whatever you see, keep your thoughts to yourself. As the driver said, I'd better warn you I'm not doing it if it's not above board, he had produced his card; he wouldn't have one the next day. Don't worry, I'm a policeman, what we're going to do is perfectly legal.

Off they went. He sat in the back giving instructions. The first stop was an EDF[1] footbridge over the A4 crossing the Seine. He had already patrolled that area and under the concrete approach leading up to the bridge there was always a horde of down-and-outs lying night and day on pieces of rotting mattress. He said, stop there, I'll be back, and flashed his torch all round. Police, you in there, up you get, what sort of time do you think this is? Two eyes dazzled by the light gazed back at him in total bewilderment, but before the tramp had time to react he got out a wad of notes. I've decided to give you a subsidy, a special subsidy. Three thousand francs. And he gave the same to the one behind him who was also showing signs of life. Here you are, mate, don't waste it. As they set off again in the taxi he went into

---

[1] *Electricité de France*, the French electricity board.

fits of laughter. Feeding the hungry, ha. Well at least this evening they've had a hand-out.

The black taxi-driver tried to remain impassive, but it wasn't easy. They drove back towards Paris and the cop asked him to keep to the outer boulevards of the city in the direction of the Porte Dorée. At each bus-stop he halted, lowered his window, and held out a banknote to the waiting prostitutes. It's Father Christmas, my dear, courtesy of the police force. At the Porte de Vincennes they took a left turn and were going back up the road when a squad of plainclothes police cut them off: four young men in leather jackets. One of the girls must have talked because the inspector asked him, Are you the madman dishing out all the cash? He remained calm. Very calm. I'm in the force, old chap. The money's mine and I do what I want with it. I'm retiring today, and if I feel like chucking my money away that's my business, I don't see you've got any reason to say anything. The young men looked at him, flabbergasted. Is it true you've been slipping them banknotes? To the whores? To the junkies? The oldest one was aghast. And you're in the police? You're a cop and you're throwing money at them? The other remained expressionless. I do what I like with my money. I shall give it away if I feel like it.

They were off again, the cop more and more pleased with himself and the driver frankly amazed but nonetheless amused. Your mates thought you were crazy, they don't often see the likes of you.

In the Rue de Bagnolet he went into a small seedy café full of drunks and, without ordering anything, came straight to the point. What's your opinion of the police, then? Do you think they're all bastards? And a drunk said yes, they must be or they would all be working in the clinics, they wouldn't be cops. The café owner, somewhat ill at ease, realized the question was a bit odd, and played for time. It depends, sometimes they're quite decent. But the large majority of customers agreed that they were rats and dirty bastards. The cop nodded his head thoughtfully, and showed them his card. Rats and dirty bastards, eh? The owner was white, but before he was allowed to open his mouth and explain, that's not what they meant to say, Monsieur le Commissaire, the other had his hands already full of 500-franc banknotes. Come on now, whose turn is it? Who wants a bit of cash? I've got loads, I've brought it for you. For the first few seconds there was no reaction, but when he repeated, Come on now, be brave, it won't eat you, the small party of drunks mobbed him. Ah, food for the hungry, the hungry and the winos.

Near Stalingrad the driver asked, Where are we going now? And he said go right round the other side till we get to the end of the Rue d'Aubervilliers. Groups of West Indians more decrepit than a Bronx nightmare were hanging out in various parts of Tout-Va-Mieux. The driver looked at him in the mirror. What are you intending to do now? Not help those animals out?

He approached the group and, banknotes in hand, said Psssst! And the rabble threw themselves upon him, give it here, here, and he threw notes at them, 500, 200 francs. No one said a word or asked the meaning of this madness: who was this great burly chap in an overcoat, with greying hair, throwing his money away on the corner of the Boulevard de la Villette at two in the morning one freezing night in January?

Animals, the driver said, starting the car again. When I think there's a lot of them out there who come from my country it makes me feel real bad.

At Marx-Dormoy the policeman said, We'll stop once more at the Porte de Clignancourt for five minutes and then you drop me at the Gare du Nord.

It was almost three o'clock and it had begun to snow. Under the railway bridge, on the Boulevard Ney, there were still two prostitutes, looking frozen, like emaciated mummies in their tights with their front teeth half broken and covered with lipstick. My God, the driver said, how on earth do they get in that state? The policeman's bag was almost empty, only a few tens of thousands of francs left. He gave some money to the driver—here, take these before I'm broke—and went to see to the two girls. What's your name?, he asked. On the boulevard people were driving slowly because of the snow, to avoid skidding. The girl didn't answer. It's a hundred for a blow-job. Intercourse is two hundred and more if you don't use a condom. He held out a huge wad. For you and your friend. The girl looked at him uncomprehendingly.

Take it, it's for you. Aren't you behind with the rent? Don't you owe your pimp money? The girl said yes. Well then, here you are, it's for you, you and your friend.

Feeding the hungry.

Animals.

Ignorant, starving animals.

As it was getting light, in the train which was taking him home, he was still laughing about it. Feeding the hungry, my word, what a great night it had been. What a truly wonderful night.

Notes on the Authors

Guy de Maupassant (1850–93), though in many ways associated in his writings with Normandy, nevertheless wrote several stories situated in or around Paris. Two are included here. Maupassant published sixteen volumes of short stories in his lifetime. After a suicide attempt at the beginning of 1892, he spent the last eighteen months of his life in a mental home in Passy, in Paris.

Gérard de Nerval (the pseudonym of Gérard Labrunie, 1808–55) was born in Paris. This story is one of three *Contes et Facéties*, witty or satirical little stories especially popular between the fifteenth and eighteenth centuries; this might be appropriately characterized as a *conte fantastique*, a popular genre at the time. The *conte fantastique* originated in Germany and usually had as its subject a supernatural phenomenon, to which the author attempted to give some psychological basis. Nerval, a poet and visionary writer, was mentally unstable. He hanged himself from a railing in the Rue de la Vieille Lanterne in an old *quartier*, demolished in 1855, in the Châtelet area of modern Paris.

Honoré de Balzac (1799–1850) is chiefly known for his prodigious output of writing about society in Paris and the provinces in *La Comédie humaine*. This story, which appeared in 1830, is possibly a first draft of a novel, and one of several stories or 'tableaux' originally published in the magazine *La Caricature*. The Palais-Royal area at that time was both fashionable and seedy.

Émile Zola (1840–1902) was born in Paris and settled there from 1858 onwards. He is noted mainly for his cycle of twenty novels about the Rougon-Macquart family, several of which (in particular *Le Ventre de Paris*, about the famous market in Les Halles) depict life and society in the slums of Paris in the nineteenth century. The story from *Contes et Nouvelles* (1865–72) included here is more of a satirical reflection upon the nature of squares than a conventional narrative.

Sidonie-Gabrielle Colette (1873–1954) was brought to Paris from Burgundy by her first husband, who published under the name 'Willy'. Colette wrote prolifically about Paris literary and artistic society. She performed in music-hall in Paris and later lived for several years in an apartment in the Palais-Royal gardens. In these sketches of Montmartre and the Bois de Boulogne, her love of the countryside, which she never lost, is evident.

Michel Butor (born 1926), a poet and well-known practitioner of the *nouveau roman*, experimented with new forms of narrative. This series of impressionistic sketches of the Gare Saint-Lazare, from his collection *Illustrations*, is typical of his work.

Léon-Paul Fargue (1876–1947), a poet, was born and brought up in Paris. He is famous for his essays and memoirs of Paris, especially *Le Piéton de Paris* (1939), which provides an interesting documentation of life in the city. The sketch included here is from *Les XX arrondissements de Paris*, which evokes each area in turn.

Julien Green (1900–98) was a novelist who had American parents but was born and brought up in Paris and wrote in French. During the Second World War, from the Occupation to the Liberation, he lived in the United States.

Maryse Condé (born 1937) is a Francophone writer, critic, and professor from Guadeloupe. She has published in a wide variety of literary genres. This largely autobiographical story demonstrates the social commitment and concerns that characterize her writings.

Georges Perec born in Paris in 1936 has written frequently on the city, often in an experimental way. The story here is a more traditional reconstruction of an episode in his childhood.

Roger Grenier (born 1919) is the author of many novels and short stories. He spent his childhood in southwest France and came to Paris in the Second World War, working with Camus after the Liberation. He is an editor at Gallimard.

Andrée Chedid was born in Cairo in 1920 and completed her secondary education in Paris, where she has lived since 1946. She is widely known for her poetry, as well as for her stories and novels.

Didier Daeninckx, born in Saint-Denis, in 1949 is a writer and journalist now living in the Paris suburb of Aubervilliers. He is well known as a writer of *romans policiers*, and has won many prizes for his work, including the Prix Goncourt du Livre de Jeunesse.

Jacques Réda (born 1929) has written several books of essays and stories about different areas of Paris, including *Les Ruines de Paris*. This essay is taken from a series called *Le Quinzième Magique* in *Châteaux des courants d'air*.

Jean Echenoz, born in Orange, in 1948 achieved immediate and remarkable success with this story, '*L'Occupation des Sols*', based in the Canal Saint-Martin area of Paris, and published in 1988. In 1999 he won the prestigious Prix Goncourt for his novel, *Je m'en vais*.

Annie Saumont was born in Cherbourg in 1927. After she left school she moved to Paris and worked as a translator. She has published a dozen volumes of short stories, many written in her characteristically colloquial style. She has won many prizes for them, including the Prix Goncourt and the Prix Renaissance.

Cyrille Fleischman, a Jewish writer born in Paris in 1941, writes principally about the Marais area, the fourth *arrondissement*. In 1995 he won an Academy prize for his collection of stories, *Les Nouveaux Rendez-vous au métro Saint-Paul*.

Anna Gavalda was born in Boulogne-Billancourt in 1970. She taught for some years in a secondary school before winning a short-story prize in Melun in 1997. The book from which this story is taken, *Je voudrais que quelqu'un m'attende quelque part*, has been translated into nineteen languages.

Frédéric Beigbeder was born in Neuilly-sur-Seine in 1965. He had his first real literary success with *Mémoires d'un jeune homme dérangé* in 1990. His latest novel, *99 Francs* (whose title has now amusingly been changed to 14,99 Euros), published by Grasset, is a satire on the advertising industry. He is closely associated with the Saint-Germain area of the Latin Quarter.

Hugo Marsan, novelist and short story writer was born in Dax in 1944 and now lives in Paris. As a child he was much influenced by his grandmother in Les Landes. He gave up teaching in order to write and helped establish the magazine *Nouvelles Nouvelles*. His most recent book of short stories is *Place du Bonheur* (Mercure de France, 2001), in which this story appears.

Vincent Ravalec was born in Paris in 1962 and has always lived in or around the city. He left school at fourteen. His first collection of stories was published by Le Dilettante, and the context for his work is nearly always Parisian. He is well known as a film-maker as well as a writer.

Further Reading

Reference books and books about Paris

Paris, Guides Bleus, Harrap (1991). This is probably the most comprehensive guide to Paris, with a wealth of useful background information, detailed history, and maps.

Paris par arrondissement, Editions L'Indispensable (1988), a useful pocket guide for getting around the capital.

Dictionnaire Historique des Rues de Paris (2 volumes), ed. Jacques Hillairet, (Les Editions de Minuit 1997). These two volumes contain detailed histories of each street and the buildings in them as well as photographs of streets in Paris in different decades.

Au fil des lignes du métro, by Dan Sylvestre (Hors série no. 2, L'Itinérant, 1997). This booklet contains a fascinating potted history of each métro station.

Eugène Atget's Paris, by Andreas Krase, ed. Hans Christian Adam (Taschen, 2001). Photographic evidence of what Paris looked like in the first two decades of the twentieth century.

The Streets of Paris, by Richard Cobb, with photographs by Nicholas Breach (Duckworth, 1980). What Paris looked like in the last two decades of the twentieth century.

The Time Out Book of Paris Walks, ed. Andrew White (Penguin, 1999)

Les Nouveaux Mystères de Paris, by Léo Malet, published in the 1950s and available now in French in Pocket Classiques.

Each detective story takes place in a different *arrondissement* of Paris.

Anthologies of French short stories

The Oxford Book of French Short Stories, ed. Elizabeth Fallaize (OUP, 2002).

The Time Out Book of Paris Short Stories, ed. Nicholas Royle (Penguin, 1999). These are mainly by Anglophone writers.

XciTés, ed. Georgia de Chamberet (Flamingo, 1999). A selection of stories and extracts from novels by twentieth-century French writers in the 1980s and 1990s.

French Short Stories, vols 1 and 2, eds. Pamela Lyon and Simon Lee (Penguin, 1966 and 1972).

Short Stories in French, New Penguin Parallel Text, trans. and ed. Richard Coward (Penguin, 1999). These are bilingual texts and therefore useful for language students.

On the short story

The Short Story, by Ian Reid, in *The Critical Idiom*, ed. John T. Jump (Methuen, 1977).

La Nouvelle française contemporaine, by Annie Mignard (Ministère des Affaires etrangères, 2000). This is in three languages and has a helpful list of short-story writers.

Websites

On *arrondissements* and *quartiers*:
www.pariserve.tm.fr/quartier/decouvre.htm
www.frumious.demon.co.uk/paris3.html

On the métro:
www.paris.org.metro

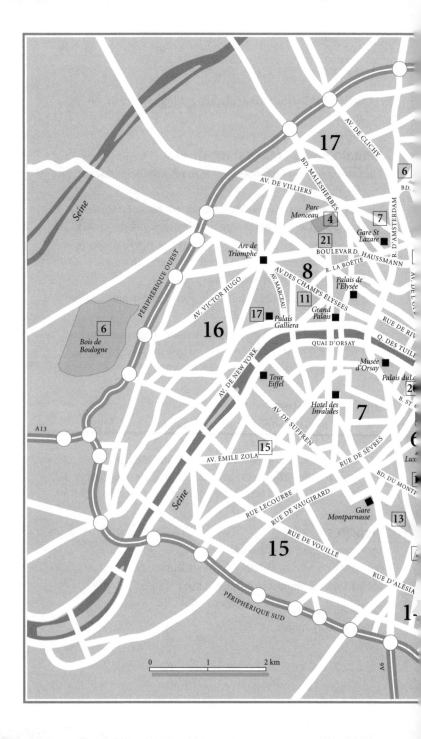

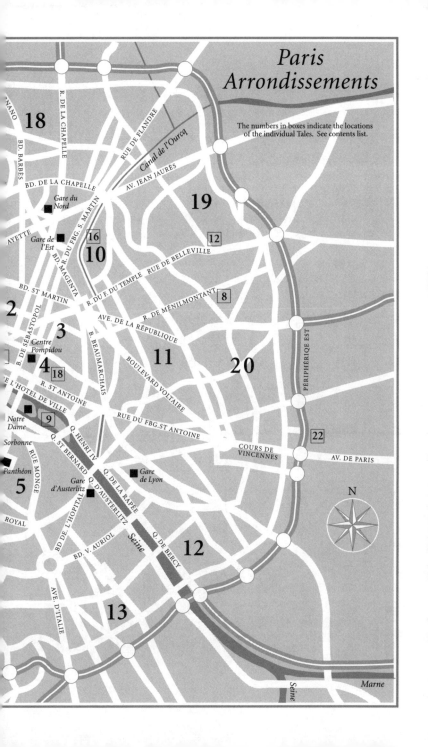

Paris Arrondissements

The numbers in boxes indicate the locations of the individual Tales. See contents list.

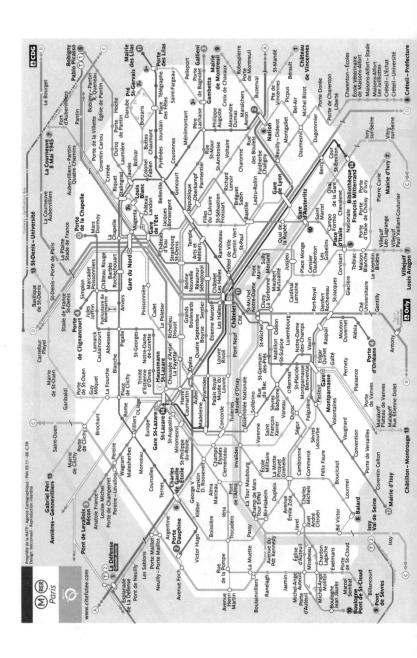